The Memory Prisoner

The Memory Prisoner

by

THOMAS BLOOR

Dial Books for Young Readers

NEW YORK

First published in the United States 2001
by Dial Books for Young Readers
A division of Penguin Putnam Inc.
345 Hudson Street
New York, New York 10014

Published in Great Britain 2000
by Hodder Children's Books
Copyright © 2000 by Thomas Bloor

Designed by Nancy R. Leo-Kelly
Text set in Berthold Baskerville
Printed in the U.S.A. on acid-free paper
1 3 5 7 9 10 8 6 4 2

Library of Congress Cataloging-in-Publication Data
Bloor, Thomas, date.
The memory prisoner / by Thomas Bloor.
p. cm.
Summary: When her younger brother is in danger, fifteen-year-old Maddie
runs out of the house she has not left since she was two years old.
ISBN 0-8037-2687-2
[1. Recluses–Fiction. 2. Brothers and sisters–Fiction. 3. Librarians–Fiction.]
I. Title.
PZ7.B62365 Me 2001   [Fic]–dc21   00-060254

For Elaine,
Joanna,
and Louise

The Memory Prisoner

Chapter 1

Maddie had not left the house for thirteen years. Not once. Not since she visited the public library with her grandad. The day after their visit the library shut and never reopened. Some time later, Maddie's mother told her that Grandad Lemon had died. Maddie stayed in the house from then on and nothing anyone said could dislodge her.

Maddie remembered that night quite clearly, despite being only two at the time. It was her first memory. And Maddie had a memory like a steel trap. Once something had been caught there, it could never escape. Maddie herself came to view this as a curse. There were many gray mornings when the empty week ahead and the empty week behind linked all the other empty weeks together in an endless, unbroken chain. On such mornings Maddie would sit at her window, forcing her hips into the old wicker armchair, feeling it creak and groan under her weight, and she would sigh and say aloud:

"Maddie Palmer, your memory keeps you a prisoner. What good is a memory you can't control? What if there's something you really need to forget?"

It was the same thing she told the doctor on the one occasion he visited. She was eight. She had refused to leave the house for the past six years. She sat in the wicker chair, which still seemed roomy in those days, and she swung her big boulder of a face around to look at him. Dr. Deans stood in the doorway and spoke to Maddie from there.

"Why won't you leave the house, Maddie?" he asked, his voice a throaty wheeze.

"I can't. It's my memory, you see."

"Your memory?" the doctor asked, coughing quietly into his fist.

"Yes. I can't forget. So I can't leave the house."

"What can't you forget, Maddie?" the doctor gasped, his eyes streaming.

"I don't know."

"But, Maddie, I thought you said you couldn't forget."

"That's right," Maddie sighed irritably, "but I don't know what it is I can't forget. The nearest I can get to forgetting it is to put it away somewhere in the back of my memory, like hiding something on a shelf out in the shed or somewhere so you don't have to look at it. Do you see?"

Maddie looked hard at the doctor, who was shifting from foot to foot, standing in the doorway.

"No," he said, "not really. Still, I believe social services will be satisfied that you cannot attend school on . . . er . . . medical grounds."

There was a silence. Then Maddie said, "Are you ill?"

"Allergy," said Dr. Deans. Soon he left.

But Keith, who had been listening and watching from his favorite place, lying on his stomach underneath the table, came crawling out, his elbows furry with dust, and stood quietly in front of his older sister.

"What do you want?" snapped Maddie.

"I get it, Mad," he said.

"What are you talking about, Keith?"

"I get what you mean, Mad, about that thing, you know, that you want to forget but you can't, so you put it on like a shelf in the back of your mind." Keith came to a halt and looked at his feet.

"Well," said Maddie, smoothing the fabric of her cotton dress across her stomach. She sniffed, then continued, "It's nice to know *someone* understands. But, Keith . . ."

Keith looked up.

"Don't ever call me Mad again."

Chapter 2

"Mad Maaaaaaddie! Oh, mental mental Maaaaaaddie! Mad, mad, mad, Maaaaaaaaaad!"

So sang Park beneath the window. He sang with a mocking sweetness. He had the voice of an angel. His face, too, had angelic qualities. But his eyes–long-lashed, big, and blue–betrayed the shallow waters of his soul. They showed no pity, no kindness. They were lit up by cruelty. Nothing else.

Maddie, now fifteen years old and a towering mountain of a girl, had never seen Park's eyes. For one thing, she never left the house and he was never invited in. And for another, she made it a point never to actually look at him. She sat serenely in her upstairs window, gazing out at the street below. Not once did she appear to notice her tormentors. No matter how cruel the taunts of Park and his gang, no matter how vile the lyrics of his serenading, Maddie sat unmoved, looking through them. It was as if they were not there at all.

As the light began to fade, Maddie watched the street lamp. She was watching for the exact moment that the lamp flickered on. It was controlled by a light-sensitive filament that switched on the power when the daylight had sufficiently faded. Over the years Maddie had become an expert judge of the moment she had named "The Time of the Light in the Darkness."

It was a still, cold January afternoon that, despite its bleakness, at least carried some hints of the distant spring. The sky was clear. Maddie watched its color shift, when the orange streetlight sputtered into life, from slate blue to indigo. A blackbird perched on a telegraph pole sang a sad, end of the day song, paying Park and his sniggering friends as little attention as Maddie did.

"Well, Maddie Palmer," she said aloud, "here you are again, still a prisoner of the old memory. Quite a satisfying Time of the Light in the Darkness tonight. Judged it to the nanosecond, I do believe."

She turned from the window as Keith came into the room.

"You look awful," she said. "What on earth happened to you?"

Keith, small, thin, with a thickening lip and a bloodied tissue held to his swollen nose, and looking much younger than his twelve years, came quietly into the room. He stood under the light while his sister tutted and sighed and fussed over his battered face. She did not ask him again what had happened. She waited. Although she felt an aching, helpless anger at his condition, she still waited. It was by no means unusual for him to come home with a bloody nose.

"My poor old Eyes and Ears," she said, dabbing at his nostrils with a clean handkerchief, "you're looking pretty bedraggled. If this goes on much longer, I shall have to rename you my Black Eyes and Cauliflower Ears!"

Maddie made her way out of the room and delicately picked a path down the steep, narrow staircase. It was a hazardous operation. Maddie was extremely large and had to maneuver her way around the house with great caution. This was made considerably harder by the bizarre attitude to storage adopted by her mother. Mrs. Palmer had an inexplicable hatred of cupboards and drawers. She used the stairs, the landing, and the floor space of all the rooms downstairs for storage. As Maddie descended the staircase, she passed pair after pair of boots, piles of crockery, towers of half-used paint cans, and a collection of plastic buckets stacked one inside another.

She reached the ground floor a little out of breath but without any major alarms. She threaded her way past a mountain range of cardboard boxes to reach the refrigerator in the kitchen. Mrs. Palmer came twitching in behind her.

"Now don't get everything everywhere. Mmm, yes, mmm, yes. What are you after in there? Mmm, yes . . ."

Maddie glanced over at her mother. She was a tiny woman, thin like Keith, with the same startled shock of sandy hair. Her skin was a raw, mottled pink and she moved with the frantic, jerky movements of a nervous sparrow.

"Keith's really worked up," said Maddie flatly. She pulled a tray out from under a heap of plastic bags on top of the refrigerator and began loading it with provisions. A loaf of bread, margarine, a greasy jar of crunchy peanut butter, and two pint bottles of milk. She also banged out the contents of the ice tray onto a plate and added that as well.

"We'll be eating upstairs, Mom."

"Mmm, yes? Well, don't make a mess, mind! And mind my boots on the stairs. Mmm, yes, yes, yes."

And Mrs. Palmer scuttled over to the sink and began

rummaging through a pile of old curtains heaped up on the draining board.

Upstairs again, Maddie let herself fall backward onto her bed. A great clamor of protest arose from the mattress springs. She wallowed in the sunken center of the old bed. Keith, perched on the edge, seemed to make no impression on the mattress whatsoever, as if he were as light as dust.

"Well then, my poor Eyes and Ears," Maddie said, "tell me all you've seen and all you've heard since last I lay here and you sat there."

"Since last night? Or just since this morning?"

"We can skip back to the day later, but start with your recent difficulties."

Keith bowed his head.

"Was it Park again?" Maddie asked quietly.

"Yes," Keith's reply was almost inaudible, barely more than a sigh.

"Oh, Keith! You've just got to forget it. You know how I feel about them! They can't touch me, Keith. They're out there and I'm in here! I hear them, but I don't listen. I see them, but I don't bother to look. I'm safe. You're the one who needs standing up for, not me."

"I hate them, though, Maddie. I hate the things they

say about you! And I can't just forget it. I have to tell them how I feel!" Keith shook with anger as he said this, his tiny body wracked with tension.

Maddie sighed. As usual she found herself wondering how such a mouse-like creature as her brother could have such a lion-like heart. "All right, Keith. I suppose you're doing it for yourself as much as for me," she said. "It doesn't make me feel less guilty, though. Here, put some ice on your bruises–there's some on the tray."

Maddie shifted her weight on the bed.

"Now, while you're doing that, perhaps you could think back to this morning and share your school day with me."

And so, in his small, hesitant voice, Keith told Maddie about his day. He told her everything. Every word the teacher had spoken, all the snatches he had overheard from his classmates' conversations. Everything he had read or written. He was able to remember it all, and he recited it now for his sister's entertainment.

Maddie hurried him over the parts that did not interest her and questioned him for more details about the things that did, like the whispered classroom arguments of a particularly headstrong group of girls. Their daily feuds and friendship pacts were a seething illustration of a raw struggle for power, and they fascinated Maddie.

So vividly did Keith's verbal transcripts conjure up the school life of these girls that she felt as if she knew them as well as they knew each other. As for their home lives, of which Keith could tell her nothing other than what they happened to mention at school, Maddie made up the details herself, filling notebook after notebook with descriptions of their bedrooms, parents, siblings, pets, hobbies, and extensive wardrobes.

"Keith," Maddie said, spreading her thick fingers to accept a slice of bread, slicked with peanut butter, that Keith had prepared and now passed over to her, "don't you think it might be a good idea to make some friends of your own at school? Maybe if you did, you'd have someone to stand up for you against Park and those little snot-nosed sidekicks of his."

Keith was silent for a moment. He took a tiny bite out of his half slice of bread and margarine, nibbling at it with his front teeth.

"How?" he said.

"I don't know, I've never tried it, but it can't be that difficult, can it? I mean, can't you just go up to someone and talk to them?"

Keith put down his bread.

"You don't know what it's like," he said. "I never know what to say."

"Well, you don't have any problem talking to *me*."

"That's different. I always know what you want to hear." Keith grinned suddenly. "You just want to hear everything!"

Maddie sighed. "Everything. That's true . . ." She took a bite of her bread and chewed.

"Well then, my dear old Eyes and Ears," she said, "tell me everything again. You can start with what Kelly Anderson was wearing today."

It was The Time of the Light in the Darkness once again. Maddie was watching the streetlight and waiting for Keith. She heard his scuffling footsteps on the path and glanced down, missing the moment when the light came on.

"I hope you've got some good stuff to tell me today, Eyes 'n' Ears," she said. "I missed The Time of the Light in the Darkness tonight and it was all your fault." Maddie tugged herself out of the wicker chair and stood with her back to the window, smoothing her skirt across her stomach.

"What's the matter?" Maddie looked hard at Keith. There were no signs of violence, but he was shivering and staring at the floor.

"Are you ill?" Maddie said.

"Everything's changed, Maddie!" Keith blurted out. "He's taken me out of school. He said he's in charge of my education from now on. But, Maddie—I don't want to go there!" Keith's normally quiet voice was raised, edged with a tremor of panic.

"Keith, what are you talking about? Go where?"

"To the library! To the Tower Library!"

Chapter 3

Maddie placed her hands on Keith's shoulders. She felt his tiny frame buckle a little under the weight.

"And who says you have to go to the Tower Library?"

"Mr. Lexeter." Keith's voice fell to a sullen whisper and he looked at the ground.

"Lexeter? The head librarian?"

"Yes. He says I've been selected. He says I'm to be schooled in the ways of the Tower Library. He wants me to grow up to be his right-hand man." Keith sounded as if he would rather die.

"But how did he come to choose you?" Maddie asked, bewildered.

"Because of that stupid exam he made all the schools give us. I came out on top. He thinks I'm a genius," Keith said miserably.

"Tell me," said Maddie firmly. "Tell me everything."

So Keith told her everything.

He began with Lexeter's arrival in the school. The booming voice of the principal, laughing too loudly, nervously showing this important visitor to the classroom door. Keith heard his name spoken as the principal whispered to Miss Barnes, seated at her desk at the front of the classroom. He glanced up to see the two of them talking, their eyes swiveling in his direction, heads nodding while Mr. Lexeter stood in the doorway, his head stooped over at the neck as if from long years of looking down on all the world.

Mr. Lexeter was the most important man in Pridebridge. Maddie knew as much as any other Pridebridge resident about Mr. Lexeter, probably more. She read the *Pridebridge Weekly Exchange,* a local newspaper that Mrs. Palmer bought on Thursday mornings. Maddie had taught herself to read and write with the *Pridebridge Exchange.* It was the only reading matter she ever had. Mrs. Palmer would not have books in the house. She said they put her in mind of bookcases, and she could not stand that.

By Thursday afternoon, every week, Maddie had

read the *Exchange* from cover to cover. Since she never forgot anything she read, she could, at will, recall the names and faces of all the newlywed couples; the facts of every reported burglary, traffic offense, or late-night scuffle; the details of the Town Council's clean up after your pet campaign; the results of the Pridebridge inter-schools football league. And every one of the countless reports regarding Mr. Lexeter: Mr. Lexeter attending council meetings, Mr. Lexeter explaining again the impossibility of reopening the library to the general public, Mr. Lexeter emphasizing the importance of the Tower Library as *"an international center for academic study, drawing professors and intellectuals from all around the world to seek admittance to its exclusive membership."*

She knew his face, gaunt and unsmiling, with its snout-like nose and shiny forehead, from countless grainy newspaper photographs. For Maddie there was a horrible sense of the familiar about that face that she could never fully explain. She knew the way he stood too, stoop shouldered but still a head taller than the nervously grinning town officials or deputy librarians with whom he was usually pictured. She knew the public face of Lexeter, and she did not like it.

"I don't like Lexeter!" Maddie snorted. "I don't like him one little bit! Sorry, Keith, carry on."

Keith carried on. His voice was quiet and hesitant, his

language sometimes awkward, and yet Maddie was always able to enter into his descriptions as if she were hearing the words of a master storyteller. As he muttered and coughed his way through the details of how he had been taken to the principal's office to be spoken to by the eminent librarian, to Maddie it was almost as if she had been there herself. In her mind's eye she saw Park's mocking angel's leer as Keith stumbled out of the classroom. She saw the sweating dome of the bald principal, seated in his office, smelled his coffee breath, felt his nervousness in the presence of the mighty Lexeter. And she saw the head librarian in his gray coat and black scarf, his face long and drawn, his shiny skin a livid pink.

He spoke in a tone of voice that expressed his intense irritation at the fact that he had to talk at all, especially to people who were so far beneath his station in life.

"You are to report to the Tower Library tomorrow morning at eight o'clock sharp. Press the buzzer. You will be admitted."

Lexeter sketched the pretense of a smile. "You should consider yourself very lucky."

"Oh, yes indeed!" the principal gushed. "Oh, most certainly yes, Mr. Lexeter, it really is a very great honor! Young Keith is a credit to Pridebridge High School!"

Lexeter gave the principal a cold stare.

"Well. He is no longer a pupil at this school. He belongs to the Tower Library now. He will receive the highest quality education. I shall personally see to it. Few are privileged to be admitted to my library. I hope that I shall not regret seeking a Pridebridge child as library apprentice. I would hate to see the school lose out."

At this Lexeter gave the principal a meaningful look. The principal spluttered into his coffee, overturned his cup, spilling dregs onto his pants, and leaped to his feet.

"Oh, no, sir! You really, most certainly, will not regret it!" he almost shouted. "No, not for a moment," he went on. Then he turned to Keith, a desperate smile on his face.

"Mr. Lexeter won't regret it, will he, Keith?"

Keith looked from the principal to Lexeter and back again. He could not decide which of them horrified him the most.

Chapter 4

Keith was droning through a description of his journey back from school when Mrs. Palmer came twitching into Maddie's bedroom.

"Oh, Keithy, mmm, yes, mmm, you have really gone and done it now, haven't you! Tower Library apprentice! I didn't know there *was* such a thing!"

"I think Keith is the first one." Maddie spoke from the bed, where she had gone to recline during Keith's description of his day.

Mrs. Palmer began patting at Keith's hair.

"Your hair needs a wash, Keithy. And you'll wear your corduroy jacket tomorrow, mmm, yes?"

"Oh, Mom!"

"Don't you 'oh, Mom' me, mmm, yes!"

Keith shot Maddie an apologetic look and then slipped quickly out of the room.

"And make sure you give yourself a bath too!" his mother shouted after him. She remained in Maddie's room for a few moments, jogging from one foot to the other, fidgeting with the strings of the threadbare apron she had on, a pulse fluttering in her throat. Maddie, still lying beached upon the bed, eyed her mother in silence.

"Ooh, Maddie, mmm, yes." Mrs. Palmer moved toward the door. "I don't know how you can bear that wardrobe. And the chest of drawers too, mmm, yes, I really don't know how you put up with them!" And with that she went twitching out of the room.

Maddie heaved herself out of bed at half past seven the next morning. She picked her way down the cluttered stairway to see Keith off on his first day at the Tower. She stood at the foot of the stairs, her voluminous yellow nightgown billowing around her. Keith stood by the open front door, looking at Maddie through red-rimmed eyes while Mrs. Palmer twittered in the background.

"Good-bye," he said, his voice no more than a whisper.

"Oo, now, Keithy, you sound as if you're never coming home again, mmm, yes! See you later. You mind how you go. Yes, yes, mmm."

"You tell me all about it, Eyes and Ears," said Maddie. "Until The Time of the Light in the Darkness, brother?"

Keith blinked and forced a smile.

"Okay, Maddie," he said.

And then he was gone, leaving the front door open. Maddie stood for a while, staring out into the street. She felt, as she always did when confronted by an open door, as if she were standing on the edge of a precipice overlooking a bottomless ocean. A strong wind gusted into the house, ruffling Maddie's hair, tugging at her nightgown. Mrs. Palmer scurried around her daughter and closed the door.

Maddie paced her bedroom floor for much of the day. The floorboards sighed and creaked in a rhythmic pattern as she marked out the same small circuit, from wardrobe to chest of drawers to bed and back, time and time again.

It was all so sudden. She had lost Keith's tales from Pridebridge High School, his reports of lessons, of stories, of gossip overheard and friendships observed at a distance. She had lost Kelly Anderson and the other girls in her brother's class. But what would Keith bring her instead, when the street lamp flickered to life outside her window?

"Mad Maaaaaadie! Oh, mad, mad Maaaaaaadie!" Park yodeled, unseen below the window. Maddie looked across the street to the crumbling chimneys and grass-clogged gutters of the deserted building that stood, life-less in the fading afternoon light, opposite the Palmers' home. It had once been the town's post office. It had been closed for years now, ever since the sorting of the town mail had been taken over by the Tower Library.

Maddie let a sigh escape her lips. She spoke aloud, her own voice filling the small bedroom, reassuring and familiar. She had been talking to herself for years.

"Well, well. I see they've let the little children out of school."

Park's voice floated up from the street.

"But, soft! What light through yonder window breaks? It is—Ouch!" His mocking Shakespearean speech was cut off abruptly and the jeering laughter of the rest of his gang turned to angry shouts.

With the barest tipping of her head, Maddie glanced down into the street. Keith stood on the other side of the road with the lamppost at his back. He held a clump of earth in his fist, which he must have pulled up from the neglected and overgrown grounds of the old post office.

Another clump lay at Park's feet. Park himself was bent double with one hand clamped against the side of his head. His reddening face was contorted with pain and fury.

"Get him!" he shouted, pointing a shaking finger across the street to where Keith stood, still and silent. There were two other boys with Park. One was short with white-blond hair and a permanent slack-jawed, wet-lipped grin. The other was taller, with a ruddy complexion, his cropped hair doing nothing to hide two crimson, greasy-looking ears. Both boys had the blank, dead-eyed stare of killer sharks, and they now directed their gaze toward Keith.

The blare of a power horn and the roar of a diesel engine alerted the boys to the fast-approaching eighteen-wheeler. It was a monstrous machine bearing down on them, each wheel the height of a man, more like a train than a truck, with its chimney stack over the cabin belching black diesel fumes into the evening air.

Park's thugs jumped back onto the pavement, their curses drowned in the shuddering earthquake of sound that accompanied the truck's passing. The taillights disappeared down the road, leaving the street shrouded in a pall of smoke. Park, now seeming to have recovered from Keith's well-aimed attack, strutted across the pavement and stepped down from the curb. Then he stopped. White Hair was looking up and down the street, blinking in disbelief. Ruddy Face stood, scratching his bottom and gawking at Park. Park himself stood stock-still in the middle of the road staring at the deserted street, the lamppost, and the post office until another blaring car horn sent him leaping back onto the pavement. For, while the three youths had waited for the first truck to pass, Keith had vanished.

Chapter 5

Maddie remained at her window staring out across the street long after Park's gang had dispersed. She saw the streetlight come on but took no pleasure in it. She waited.

At last, through the deepening gloom, she glimpsed a movement in the shadows of the post office. Keith came worming out from behind a sheet of corrugated steel that covered one of the downstairs windows. He glanced cautiously around before crossing the road and darting up the front path.

Maddie gave a sigh of relief and stood up. The wicker chair was wedged firmly onto her behind. She tutted aloud and freed herself from its embrace with a sharp, dismissive blow from the flat of her hand. The chair hit the floor and toppled over. It lay on its back by the window.

Maddie crossed to the bed and imitated the wicker chair, letting herself fall backward. Her fall was slow and relentless, like a tall building under demolition.

Keith had failed to slip past the kitchen. Mrs. Palmer had seen him. As the springs in the mattress settled, Maddie listened to the sound of her mother's voice. Mrs. Palmer was clearly trying to satisfy both her curiosity about Keith's first day at the library and, at the same time, her outrage at the state of his corduroy jacket.

It was another twenty minutes before Maddie heard Keith's soft footsteps at her bedroom door. He came in carefully, carrying a tray on which was balanced a plate piled with bread and margarine, a jar of honey, and two mugs of lukewarm cocoa.

Maddie heaved herself up onto one elbow and began ladling pools of honey onto a slice of bread with a butter knife.

"I saw you do your vanishing trick out there, Keith," she said, licking a blob of margarine off her wrist. "Very impressive. I can't wait to hear what it's like inside the old post office."

"Cold," said Keith, "and it smells."

"Okay, well, never mind that now. First I need to know about the Tower Library. Tell me all, Eyes and Ears, tell me all!"

Maddie took a big mouthful of bread and honey, and followed it with a slurp of the cocoa. She settled down to listen as Keith told her about his day.

He began with even more than his usual hesitation. Maddie listened patiently as he stammered out a list of the streets he had passed on his way and of the people that he had noticed. For Maddie this drew a vivid picture of her brother's reluctant journey to the library, tripping along the half empty streets in the dismal light of the morning, his pace getting slower and slower as he neared the dreaded destination.

By ten minutes to eight he was climbing the last few steps of the stone staircase that led up to the huge iron doors of the Tower Library. Maddie had seen photographs of the building in the local paper. But she had not realized the full effect that the colossal, inhuman scale of the main entrance could have on a small, nervous boy.

Keith described it in faltering speech, roughly estimating its dimensions. Maddie, listening to the tone of his voice, could picture him standing with shoulders hunched in the dark shadow of the main entrance, gazing up at the iron doors. The doorway was straddled by a stone arch, decorated with austere, geometric patterns. Beyond the arch, rising into the slate-colored sky like a giant finger pointed threateningly at the heavens, was the great gray tower itself.

Keith looked around for some kind of bell or door knocker or buzzer. There was none. There was not even a mailbox. After standing motionless for a few minutes, he raised his fist and tapped timidly at the cold iron door. He had not expected his knocking to be heeded, had not even expected it to be audible. However, the iron doors turned out to be hollow and as resonant as a church bell. His gentle tap was instantly magnified into a low, clamorous tolling. The sound rolled and echoed, booming inside the building.

A gust of chill wind sent a tangle of dusty twigs dancing around Keith's ankles as the echoes of his knocking died away. Silence.

A sudden voice, cutting harshly through the empty air, sent Keith spinning around with a startled cry.

"Hey! What do you think you're doing?" The speaker was a short man in a dark blue uniform, his face flushed an angry red, his thinning hair lacquered into an oily forelock that trembled above his scalp. He was standing at the foot of the stone staircase, glaring up at Keith.

"I . . . have to get in," Keith said.

"What's that?" The man started up the stairs, swinging his arms and letting out short gasping breaths.

"I need to get into the library," Keith said in a miserable whisper.

The man stood panting at the top of the stairs.

"Oh, no you don't," he wheezed. "Nobody gets in there 'cept staff." He wiped his mouth with the back of his hand.

"Mr. Lexeter told me to come here at eight o'clock," Keith said.

The man's expression changed.

"You're not that Palmer lad, are you?"

"Yes, I suppose I am."

"Well, what are you doing fooling around here then?" the man shouted, his face purple, a vein pulsing alarmingly beneath the skin at the side of his neck. "Come on. No one ever uses the main entrance, least of all snotty little apprentice librarians like you."

"I'm not," Keith said quietly as he followed the man down the steps and around the building. They were heading toward an unmarked side door fitted with an intercom buzzer and security cameras.

"Not what?"

"Snotty. I'm not snotty."

The man halted in his stride. The bunch of shiny keys, hanging from a chain on his belt, tinkled into silence.

"Oh. I see. One of *those* types, are we?" he said. "Right. I shall remember you, Palmer. One thing you'll learn here is that I don't forget easy, not me, not Rowley Potts. Oh, no. Let me give you a for instance. A big lad called Smithers used to pick on me when I was just a little boy back in kindergarten. Used to call me Roly Poly. Two weeks ago I saw him walking his dog on the grass in front of the library here. I recognized him, all right, even though I hadn't seen him for forty years. I got on the phone to the local police. Direct line to the boys in blue we have here, you know. Before Smithers knows it, he's down at the station having to talk his way out of trespassing and allowing his dog to dirty the street. So you see, I don't forget. Not Rowley Potts. Oh, no."

Potts turned to the intercom and slowly punched in the security code. The door remained firmly locked, however. Potts muttered angrily under his breath and then tried again. After his third attempt the buzzer gave a metallic bleat and he pushed open the door, standing aside with an exaggerated pretense at courtesy, to let Keith enter first.

It was gloomy inside. A buzzing strip light hung from the ceiling, its casing peppered with the shadowed bodies of countless flies. It shed a dull yellow light on a corridor that stretched away to a pair of swinging doors at the far end.

Potts lifted the bunch of keys and jiggled them in his fist.

"You have to report to Personnel," he said, and

launched into a rapid and complicated description of how to get to the personnel office. Keith, his stomach churning with nerves, could not keep his eyes off the security man's trembling curl of hair.

Potts fell into an abrupt silence. He turned his back on Keith, unlocked a narrow door marked SECURITY, and disappeared, slamming it shut behind him. It was only after Potts had gone that Keith realized he had not listened to the directions at all.

Keith stood for a few moments, alone in the corridor. He did not want to knock at the door and ask Potts to tell him again how to get to the personnel office. He set off toward the set of swinging doors. Pushing through them, he saw another pair of doors not far from the first. These were originally white but were now grimy with fingerprints and boot scuffs. Keith shouldered these grubby doors apart and felt them swing heavily together again behind him. A set of green double doors was just ahead of him.

After going through two more sets of double doors, Keith took the first turn he came to and found himself at the top of a dimly-lit stairway. He was hopelessly lost already. He needed to find someone he could ask for directions.

He listened to the scuffling of his own footsteps as he crept down the stairs. He could hear sounds from somewhere close by. A muffled thumping. As he reached the foot of the stairs and turned into another corridor, the noises grew louder. They were coming from behind a door at the far end. As he approached the door, Keith saw that it was reinforced by steel panels. A hinged grille of iron bars was fitted over the front. There was a circular shutter, a spy hole, at eye level. This was a cell door, a prison door, and the noise was being made by someone or something banging at the inside, again and again and again.

Keith came to a halt in front of the door. There was nowhere else to go except back the way he had come. It was a dead end. Suddenly, the pounding stopped. And then the heavy silence was broken by the cracked voice of a man crying out from behind the cell door:

"Nnnnooo!"

Chapter 6

Keith turned in panic and fled back up the corridor. He could hear the voice behind the door shouting hoarsely, desperately, as he ran up the stairs. He clapped his hands over his ears and closed his eyes, running blindly, two steps at a time. He ran full tilt into someone, head-butting him in the stomach. Whoever it was had stomach muscles of iron. The person didn't gasp and barely even rocked back on his heels. Keith had fallen to his knees. He opened his eyes and looked up at the gray-clad figure towering above him. It was Lexeter. The head librarian looked down, his gaze cold and unblinking.

"This area is restricted," he said. "I never want to see you in a restricted area again, do you understand?"

He walked past Keith and on down the steps without looking back. Keith began to follow.

"Mr. Lexeter! Which way is—"

Lexeter stopped so suddenly, Keith almost collided with him again and the query died on his lips. Lexeter did not turn around right away. He spoke slowly, his voice edged with an icy fury.

"I told you," he said, "that I never want to see you here again."

Lexeter then spun to face Keith. His steel gray gaze riveted Keith to the spot.

"Do I make myself clear?"

Keith nodded and backed away, stumbling up the staircase. No sound could now be heard from the prison cell below.

It was another forty-five minutes before Keith found himself standing outside the door to the personnel office. He had been wandering the corridors, passing through one set of swinging doors after another, past locked rooms and offices with no one in them, until he arrived, by chance, outside a door marked PERSON OF ICE.

Keith stared, unbelieving, at the sign until he realized that some of the white painted letters had been meticulously scraped away and that the sign had originally read PERSONNEL OFFICE. He was about to tap on the door when it was flung open from the inside and a tall woman in a shapeless brown dress walked out of the office backward, her arms full of bulging manila folders. Keith was knocked off his feet. He became entangled in the woman's legs. She trampled him with her heavy black shoes, lost her balance, and went sprawling to the cold linoleum beside him. She dropped the files and they cascaded onto the floor, bursting apart and sending reams of paper fanning out along the corridor in both directions.

Keith turned his horrified gaze upon the woman's face, expecting to find her furious. But her expression was blank. Without a word she stood up and began brushing the dust from her dress, flicking at the brown cloth with her hands as if halfheartedly shooing flies from a sugar bowl. She barely glanced at Keith, who was still on the floor.

"You must be the apprentice," she said. "My name is Miss Pring. The head librarian has asked me to oversee your work here, at least for the time being. I think we should start with some filing."

She looked squarely at him, without the least hint of a smile, and pointed to the papers scattered all over the floor.

Keith began gathering the spilled files together. Page

after page of shorthand notes written in blue ink on thin yellowish paper. There was a date, several sets of numbers, and a title typed in the top left-hand corner of every sheet. He sorted them into piles on the floor of the corridor.

Miss Pring showed Keith to a cold windowless room next to the personnel office, and then left. The walls were fitted floor to ceiling with empty shelving. There was a wooden table in the center of the room. Keith carried in the papers, piled them on the table, and then began sorting them in the way Miss Pring had explained, first according to date, then according to the various serial numbers, and then in alphabetical order according to the title written at the top of the page.

Keith sorted out five series of notes entitled "Records–Medical," six entitled "Records–Police," and three entitled "Records–Postal," but he had no idea what the shorthand notes actually said.

"Don't bother trying to read them," said Miss Pring, returning and noticing him squinting at one of the pages he was filing. "For one thing, it's none of your concern, and for another, it's all written in a specialist shorthand that is only used here at the Tower Library. Very few people know how to read it."

"Do *you* know how to?" Keith asked.

"That is my concern," said Miss Pring.

She had come to tell him that it was time for a break.

"We take a break from three-thirty until three-forty-five," she told him. "I'll show you where the staff room is."

Keith realized that he must have missed the lunch break, but he was not hungry. His mother had prepared a paper bag of food for his lunch. White bread ham sandwiches wrapped in plastic, a bottle of Coke, two packets of cookies, and a big piece of fruitcake. On the way to the library he threw the whole bag into a trash bin. Just carrying it had been making him feel ill.

He followed Miss Pring along the silent, empty corridor to a door with a frosted glass window set into it. A lace curtain, stained nicotine yellow, hung limply over the inside of the door frame. The room smelled like the ghost of burnt cabbage, tinged with stale cigarette smoke.

"You may use this mug," said Miss Pring, pointing to a chipped white cup hanging by its handle from one of a row of hooks on the wall above the porcelain sink. Several used tea bags lay in the sink, spread around the drain like drowned slugs. On the draining board there were a few packets of cocoa and coffee, and a large aluminum urn was sighing and gurgling, letting out gasps of steam from beneath an ill-fitting lid. This warm dampness from the urn was the only trace of comfort in the otherwise frosty atmosphere of the room.

Keith sat in a sag-bottomed old armchair near the door,

balancing his steaming cup of cocoa on his knee. Miss Pring selected a chair on the far side of the room and, taking a sheaf of papers from a manila folder she had brought in with her, she sat and read in silence. A wall clock up above the doorway ticktocked monotonously.

The door opened and Potts, the security man, came in. He made himself a cup of coffee, then sat down and began leafing through an old copy of the *Pridebridge Exchange*. The urn sighed mournfully. Keith cleared his throat.

"There don't seem to be many people working here. I thought there would be more," he said.

Neither Miss Pring nor Potts looked up. They both continued to read. Keith was beginning to wonder if he had actually spoken at all when Potts shifted in his chair and shook his newspaper.

"Most of 'em work up on the second floor." Potts spoke out of the corner of his mouth, with his eyes still scanning the paper in his hand. "The deputy librarians are based in the Tower. Then there are the reading rooms for the visiting academics if we ever have any. But you won't be seeing any of them. Not for a good few years. Mr. Lexeter'll want you where you can't do any damage. Ground floor is for support staff, and that's where you'll stay."

"What about the floor below, the basement?"

Potts gave a start and flung down the newspaper.

"Basement! What basement?" he spluttered, his face turning crimson. "I hope you haven't been poking around, because if I catch you where you shouldn't be . . ."

The pulse was ticking in Potts's neck. "What basement?" he shouted.

Across the room Miss Pring returned the report she had been reading to its folder.

"Keith," she said coldly, "the basement is definitely not your concern. It is now three-forty-five. Time to return to work."

Chapter 7

Darkness filled Maddie's bedroom. Keith had fallen silent. He had told her about his day. Now it was night and he was almost invisible, swathed in shadows at the foot of the bed. Maddie shifted her weight. The mattress springs sang out.

"D'you want something to eat, Keith? I'm feeling a little hungry," she said. Keith nodded.

"I won't be a minute," he said, and he slipped out of the room.

Maddie rolled onto her front and rubbed her eyes with her fists. "Oh, Keith," she said, "where *have* they sent you? What kind of a place is the Tower Library anyway? I don't like the sound of it, not one little bit!"

And then, raising her voice, she called out, "Hey, Keith! Hurry up, I'm starving! Bring the cheese, Keith! The cheese!"

But Keith returned a moment later, empty-handed. He switched the light on.

"Ow!" yelled Maddie, clapping one large hand over both eyes. "You might have warned me!"

"Sorry, Maddie. It's just that Mom's made dinner. I think we'd better go downstairs."

Maddie groaned. "What did she make?"

"Steak and potatoes."

"I just might be able to get it down," said Maddie, heaving herself off the bed.

Maddie was standing in a long, dimly-lit corridor. She knew it was a dream. It had to be; she was out of the house, so it couldn't possibly be reality. But, somehow, knowing this did nothing to lessen her fear. She took a few faltering steps along the corridor. There was a door at the far end. Now she knew where she was. This was the basement corridor at the Tower Library, just as she had pictured it from Keith's description, and ahead of her was the cell door.

She stood rooted to the spot. She felt the floor lurch beneath her feet. The corridor had become a kind of conveyor belt and she was being carried to the cell door. She tried to step backward, but something was behind her, blocking her way. Maddie was forced up against the steel grille over the door. Just in front of her eyes the cover on the small viewing slit slid open. Her face was pushed against the bars, her eye squashed up against the viewing hole. Another eye stared back, cold and unblinking.

Maddie gave a mighty shove away from the door and stumbled backward into the enveloping folds of a woven curtain. The cloth parted and she found herself outside in a sunlit garden. A figure stood there with his back to her. A tall man dressed in gray, stooped at the neck. He turned. Lexeter!

Maddie was unable to look away. She stared in horror at the head librarian. He loomed over her, swaying slightly. He seemed to be growing taller by the second. Then Maddie realized with a shock that it was the other way around. She was shrinking, getting smaller and smaller until she was no bigger than a two-year-old child.

Towering above her, Lexeter continued to sway, tipping backward and forward with increasing violence. At last he toppled. There was a splintering crash, as if an empty wardrobe had been pushed off a roof. He slammed headfirst into the ground.

Maddie gingerly approached his fallen body. She looked down. His skull seemed to have broken into pieces. And spilling out from the smashed head was a mass of worms, their tangled bodies gray and slippery in the sunshine of the garden.

Maddie clawed her way out of sleep, like a drowning swimmer forcing herself back to the surface. She emerged from the dream with a cry on her lips, a horrified yell that shattered the quiet of her bedroom.

A voice spoke in the darkness.

"It's all right, Maddie. It's all right."

"Keith?" Maddie blinked.

It was not Keith. It was Mrs. Palmer, bending over the bed, one bony hand laid awkwardly on Maddie's forehead.

"There now, mmm, yes, everything's all right. Now don't you worry, Maddie. It's all right, everything's all right."

Maddie listened to her mother's frightened, clucking voice and began to cry.

"But it isn't, Mom," she gasped between sobs. "It isn't all right!"

"Oh, Maddie!" said Mrs. Palmer. "Oh, Maddie, dear!"

When her tears had subsided, Maddie raised a hand to fish around under her pillow. She pulled out a large cotton handkerchief and blew her nose noisily.

"Mom," she said, "do you think I'll ever, you know . . . go outside again?"

" 'Course you will, dear! 'Course you will! You just

need a bit of time, that's all, to get over . . . whatever it is you've got to get over, mmm, yes."

"It's just that . . . well, sometimes I think that it would be good to visit Grandad Lemon's grave. I mean, I know he died when I was very young, but I do remember him. I think I'd like to lay a wreath or something."

"Ooh, well, Maddie, honey, I'm afraid you couldn't do that. I mean, Grandad Lemon hasn't got a grave, mmm, yes."

"Oh. You mean he was cremated?"

"Well, he would have been, yes, but they never found the body, see. Mmm, no. Never found hide nor hair of him. And there they were dragging the river for days after he disappeared. But listen to me, now. This is no way for me to talk to a girl with nightmares!"

Mrs. Palmer then embarked on a long monologue about the advantages of shopping at Saver's Paradise as opposed to Cheapo-Mart. Maddie fell back to sleep with her mother's hand still laid across her forehead and her mother's voice droning in her ear.

Chapter 8

When Maddie awoke, she was alone. The room was bathed in mid-morning sunlight. It streamed in through the open curtains. Maddie sat up in bed. The house had the still, hollow feel it had when no one else was there. Keith must have been gone for hours. And it was Thursday. Shopping day. Mrs. Palmer would be out buying potatoes and sliced white bread and tubs of margarine. She would return later that afternoon with a backache, the groceries in bulging plastic bags, and a copy of the *Pridebridge Exchange* tucked under her arm.

"Darn! I wanted to ask her some more about Grandad!" Maddie said, disrupting the silence of the house. "I always thought he died in his sleep. I'm sure that's what Mom told me. She must have been lying, to save my feelings. It's the sort of crazy thing she would do. I suppose she thinks I'm old enough for the truth now. In that case, I shall demand it! The truth, the whole truth, and nothing but the truth, as soon as she gets back from Saver's Paradise."

Maddie climbed out of bed and tiptoed through the jumble of things on the stairs on her way down to the kitchen.

"The other thing bothering me is this awful Tower Library business," Maddie announced to the empty house as she descended the staircase. "I mean, what kind of a library has all its filing written in a secret code? And, come to think of it, why isn't everything filed on computer? I thought everything was nowadays. And what about the names on those files? Medical records? Police records? The more I think about it, the odder it all sounds!"

The kitchen contained no wall cabinets or countertops. There was an old-fashioned iron stove set against one wall. But the refrigerator had now been banished to the hallway.

"I can't be in the same room with that fridge!" Mrs. Palmer had said the day she got Maddie to help her drag it out of the kitchen. "Why do they have to make them look so much like wardrobes?"

Maddie navigated her way past the kitchen's ramshackle towers of stacked-up cardboard boxes, all filled to the brim with storage jars and cans of soup, boxes of cutlery, batteries, balls of string, and other household items. She crossed to the stove and opened the heavy oven door. Warmth flooded the kitchen. A plate filled with the dried-out remnants of a cooked breakfast sat on the bottom shelf. Mrs. Palmer was determined to send Keith off to the Tower Library with a proper breakfast inside him. Keith appeared to have taken a small bite out of a piece of bread that was curling at the side of the plate. The rest had been left for Maddie. Bunching the hem of her nightie into an improvised oven glove, Maddie slid the plate out and carried it over to the kitchen table.

As she sat forking crusted baked beans and rubbery egg into her mouth, Maddie's gaze fell upon the telephone. It was in its usual place, on the floor by the door. Keith was always kicking it accidentally, sending it clattering across the tiles in a whirl of tangled cord and white plastic.

Although she had not left the house for thirteen years, Maddie had, on occasion, made telephone calls. The main thing that stopped her using the phone more often was that she had no one to call. But now a plan began to crystallize. She could use the telephone as a means to investigate the Tower Library. It was true that the town's postal duties had been taken over by the library. But what other local services were now centered behind the great iron doors of the famous Tower?

"I wonder . . ." said Maddie through a mouthful of sausage and fried tomatoes. Taking the plate of food with her, she crossed to the door and eased herself down onto her knees. She picked up the receiver and dialed Dr. Deans's number. It was at the top of a list of important phone numbers that Mrs. Palmer had scrawled, in smudged pencil, on the back of an old receipt that was thumbtacked to the wall.

The receptionist who answered the phone was reluctant at first to let Maddie speak to Dr. Deans.

"The doctor's very busy," she said with a note of finality.

Maddie took a deep breath, then subjected the woman to a merciless bombardment of hastily improvised reasons why she should, without question, be allowed to speak to the doctor. After no more than four minutes she was put through.

The doctor's voice croaked out a strangled hello before he was seized by an attack of violent choking. Maddie held the receiver away from her ear as the doctor hacked out a string of dry, painful coughs.

"Oh, hello, Dr. Deans," Maddie said when the coughing on the other end of the line had gurgled into silence.

"This is Maddie Palmer. I'm one of your patients, though, I must admit, I haven't seen you for a while."

"Maddie . . . what? Maddie who?" Dr. Deans bleated weakly.

"Maddie Palmer," she said. "I'm calling to see if you could check something for me. I'm a bit worried that I might be coming down with the mumps and I wondered if you could check my medical records and let me know if I've had them before. Maybe when I was a baby or something?"

There was silence for a moment on the other end of the line. Then the doctor had another series of dry coughs.

"Ah," he said at last, "there's a bit of a problem there, young lady. You see, all medical records, from all the practices and hospitals in the Pridebridge district, are now stored . . . er . . . centrally. We no longer have direct access to the records."

"Oh?" said Maddie. "Where are they kept, exactly?"

The doctor's voice sounded unnaturally steady as he replied. "All records are currently stored at the Tower Library."

"Oh?" said Maddie again. "Can you give me their number?"

"The number is restricted. You'll have to apply in writing."

"Okay, then," Maddie said cheerfully. "Thanks for your help."

"Palmer. Maddie Palmer," said Dr. Deans thoughtfully. "You're the housebound girl, aren't you?"

Maddie felt a tingle of unease.

"I don't know what you mean," she said.

"Yes . . . I know who you are, Maddie," the doctor wheezed, "and, Maddie, let me give you a bit of medical advice. A health warning, if you like. Where the Tower Library is concerned, it's best to leave well enough alone. Well enough alone."

And with that Dr. Deans exploded into another spluttering, chest-wrenching cough. And he was still coughing as Maddie slowly replaced the receiver.

She sat in the window paying no attention to Park's caterwauling and the forced mirthless laughter of his henchmen, White Hair and Ruddy Face. When she saw Keith's tiny figure hurrying along the pavement on the far side of the road, she stood up and pressed her face against the glass, ignoring the shrieks of mock terror from outside the house.

"Just walk past them, Keith. Pay no attention to them. Just come home. I need to speak to you, Keith. Come home!" Maddie muttered these words like a mantra, trying to will Keith to obey her and to protect him from

Park's gang by the sheer force of her mind. For a while she thought she was succeeding. Keith kept walking toward the house, Park and the others seeming to ignore him. But just as Keith started to cross the road in front of the house, the three boys suddenly charged him, fanning out to cut off any escape.

Keith had been expecting this. He sprang backward over the wall into the post office and disappeared into his hiding place behind the corrugated iron on the window. Shouting out threats and curses, Park wrenched back the iron covering and followed Keith into the gloom of the abandoned building, with Ruddy Face and White Hair close behind him.

Maddie sat helpless in her window, staring across at the blank face of the building. The street lamp fizzled alight, abruptly altering the colors and shadows of the scene before her. She could see nothing moving except the spindly grass stems that grew along the crumbling roof ledge, which were swaying in the breeze.

At last there was a movement up in one of the fourth-floor windows. It was Keith. Maddie watched him calmly clamber out through the empty window frame and carefully lower himself down the face of the building until his toes met a ledge of red brick. Here he stayed, gripping the window ledge with whitening fingertips.

Maddie held her breath. A feeling of helpless panic began to grow, churning her insides and drying out the roof of her mouth. Keith hung down below the window, spread-eagled flat against the outside wall. It was a desperate attempt to hide. Maddie leaned forward with a gasp. Park and one of his cronies had appeared on the floor below Keith's ledge, framed in a tall window. Frozen with horror, Maddie watched Park yank the latch open and push the window wide.

A visible tremor ran through Keith's body. He kicked out with his legs and tried to scramble back up to the sill. Park, meanwhile, had found a piece of timber somewhere in the building. He leaned out of the window and jabbed it at Keith's flailing legs.

Despite Park's efforts to dislodge him, Keith succeeded in dragging himself over the lip of the sill and back into the room on the fourth floor. Maddie let out a sigh of relief, clouding her bedroom window with condensation. In the time it took her to wipe the glass clear with her sleeve, Park had vanished. She bit her lip. Now that Keith was known to be on the floor above them, how long would it be before the gang cornered him?

And then she heard the noise. It started as a grinding squeal, crescendoed into a cascading rumble, and finished with an enormous, hissing sigh. Clouds of orange dust began to drift out of the many broken windows.

This was the only difference in the outward appearance of the building. But Maddie was in no doubt that something terrible had occurred inside.

Down at ground level two figures coated in dust and debris came falling out of one of the windows and staggered around amongst the broken stone and old tin cans that littered the front of the building. One was Park, bent double, coughing and spluttering. With him was Ruddy Face, holding a hand to a bloody cut on one cheek.

Park shook himself like a dog after a swim and ran a hand through his hair, sending up a cloud of filthy dust. Then he glanced up and down the street. He stepped over the wall and hurried away.

"Where you going?" Ruddy Face screamed after him, his voice cracked and desperate. "We can't just leave him. He's under all that junk. Didn't you see him fall through the floor? He's hurt! He might be . . . He could be . . . We've got to get help!"

Park did not even look back. He broke into a run, leaving Ruddy Face turning this way and that, helpless with panic, both hands held up to his head, his face streaked with blood and tears.

There was no sign of Keith.

Chapter 9

After what seemed to Maddie to be an interminably long time, Keith came clambering out of the ground-floor window.

Ruddy Face turned to him, flailing his arms.

"You've got to help! Please! My friend fell through the floor in there. He's underneath all that rubble and stuff. Please! You've got to help!"

Maddie saw Keith talking to the distraught boy. Keith was safe. It was White Hair who was still in the building. White Hair, with his slack jaw and his cruel, sneering laugh, lying buried underneath a tangled heap of broken flooring, probably badly hurt, perhaps even dead.

Maddie hesitated for a second and then she was up,

running out of her bedroom and down the stairs, sending boots, buckets, paint cans, and old china plates tumbling and sliding down the steps as she ran. She rounded the banister with a nimble turn of the ankle and was into the kitchen and snatching up the telephone before her mother, who was standing at the sink prodding at a tub of soaking laundry, had time to so much as look up.

After phoning an ambulance, Maddie climbed back over the heap of boots and buckets at the foot of the stairs and returned to her bedroom. She stood at the window. Keith and Ruddy Face were still outside the post office. The wail of the ambulance siren brought both of them running out into the road, waving frantically. A fire engine arrived shortly afterward and, finally, a police car.

The rescue was a slow affair. Maddie could see nothing of what was going on inside the building. She did see Keith and Ruddy Face, their differences forgotten, standing around anxiously, side by side. After a while a police sergeant ushered them both across the road and stood talking to them just below Maddie's window.

"All right, you two," he said, his voice stern, "you're both in deep trouble here, you know that, don't you? Running around in a deserted building has got to be one of the most stupid things you can do. Stupid! Your friend in there is lucky to be alive. He'll most probably be spending the next few months in the hospital thanks to this asinine stunt! I want to talk to both of your parents. Names and addresses, both of you!"

The sergeant had taken a notepad from his inside pocket and was looking expectantly at the two boys. Keith spoke first, but so quietly, Maddie could not catch what he said.

The sergeant heard, however, and he stared at Keith.

"Palmer, you say? Keith Palmer? The same Keith Palmer that's the Tower Library apprentice?"

Keith nodded.

"In that case, I know where to find you should I feel the need for further investigation," the sergeant said hurriedly. "Now, go home!"

Keith turned to Ruddy Face, but the policeman raised a hand. "Don't you worry about your friend here, sir," he said. "He'll be taken care of. Off you go now, sir."

Keith turned, his brows furrowed into a puzzled frown, and headed for the front door.

"Not you, sonny." The policeman laid a heavy hand on Ruddy Face's shoulder. "You come with me. You'd better get that cut seen to. Then you'll be needing a lift home in the police car, I daresay."

That night Mrs. Palmer made a truly enormous meal. A beef stew, rich and thick, boiled up in their largest saucepan. This was a dull gray dented pot as big as a car wheel, which had to be lifted two-handed even when it was empty. The reddish-brown stew with beans, gritty wheat, and globules of beef simmered in the pot as Mrs. Palmer stirred and stirred with a long-handled wooden spoon. In another pan a dozen suet dumplings dipped and bobbed in scalding water, topped by a greasy bubbling gravy.

Keith had tried to play down his involvement in the dramatic events across the road. But still his mother had been greatly alarmed by it all. She rushed straight into the kitchen and began preparing dinner. It was as if she wanted to bury all the worries of the world under a mountain of dumplings, to drown out all fear in a vast swamp of beef stew.

The laundry lay in a soggy heap, forgotten on the kitchen floor, as Maddie, Keith, and Mrs. Palmer sat down at the table to eat.

"Did you notice something, Keith, about that policeman? The way he acted after he found out you were the Tower Library apprentice?" Maddie said as she spooned another steaming ladle of stew onto her plate.

"Yes." Keith had his puzzled frown on again. "He called me 'sir.' And . . . he sounded . . . funny. Like he was scared."

"Exactly!" Maddie leaned forward, flicking her hair back to keep it out of her dinner. "I made some calls today, Keith. I called Dr. Deans first, asking about my medical records. Then I called the police, asking about when Grandad Lemon disappeared." She ignored the sharp intake of breath from Mrs. Palmer.

"Disappeared?" said Keith.

"I'll explain later. The point is, I didn't really want to find out anything. I just wanted to know about the records. They didn't like telling me the truth. And they all gave me rather sinister warnings about not meddling with things I didn't understand. But what it all boils down to is that no one I called could tell me *anything.* All records are held in the Tower Library. I rang the Town Hall as well. All council records are held in the Tower Library. The post office we know about. But what else has Lexeter taken over? The telephone company? Personal computers?"

"No. Not computers," said Keith. "I don't think he believes in computers. Or he's afraid of them or something. Anyway, there aren't any computers in the Tower Library. I read about it once, and I definitely haven't seen one there."

"Maybe that's one of the things those crusty old professors like about the Tower. I bet they get all nostalgic when they see the card index system, or whatever they use." Maddie snorted. She forked a quivering dumpling dripping with gravy up from her plate and shoveled it, whole, into her mouth.

"Maddie," said Mrs. Palmer, pushing away her own dinner plate, the contents barely touched. "It sounds to me as if you might be being a bit of a busybody... mmm, yes..."

Maddie turned a glassy-eyed stare on her mother.

"Well," said Mrs. Palmer, "never say I didn't tell you. Mmm, yes. A bit of a busybody." She picked up her plate and shuffled over to the sink, muttering under her breath.

"There's something weird about it all, don't you think?" Maddie said to Keith, ignoring her mother's interruption. "I aim to get to the bottom of this Tower Library business, and you, Keith, must be my eyes and ears as you always have been. But this time there's a purpose to our looking and listening." Maddie's own eyes were bright with excitement, her voice a breathless whisper. "Dig like a mole, Keith," she said. "See everything. Hear everything. And then tell everything to me!"

Keith said nothing. He speared a single bean with his fork and lifted it to his mouth.

"What?" Maddie said accusingly.

Keith sighed.

"You don't know what it's like, Maddie," he said.

"Oh, come on, Keith. We're onto something here, you *know* we are. There's a nasty, dark feeling in this town, some kind of evil secret locked away in that library, and we're the only ones who can hope to find the key."

Keith sighed again. He laid his knife and fork together and then pushed back his plate.

"Okay, Maddie," he said, "I'll help."

"Good!" Maddie smiled at him. "But you'll waste away if you don't eat, sweet Eyes and Ears." She reached over and pulled his plate toward her. She began to hum a happy tune, in between mouthfuls of Keith's leftover stew. She felt a surge of enthusiasm. This was the start of something. This was a beginning. She was not going to let anything spoil it. The recollection of those voices on the telephone, warning her to leave well enough alone where the Tower Library was concerned, had already been banished to one of the more distant and seldom visited parts of her memory.

Chapter 10

Dull winter passed into a springtime that was as sharp as a new blade, and the days grew longer. The Time of the Light in the Darkness got later. But Maddie found herself gazing at the streetlight less and less. Her life had changed. Whereas once she had watched the seasons turn, noting the minute details of moss on the window ledge, or grass in the gutters of the post office, marking each gradual change with the patient air of someone who was not going anywhere, resigned to her own inactivity, now she chafed at the slow, slow grinding of time. She had shaken off the cloak of despair that had once covered her, only to find herself shivering in the chill wind of possibilities that the library mystery presented.

She spent her days poring over her notes, waiting for Keith to return. He was the main source of the torrent of information about the Tower Library that Maddie was determined to use, to understand. Her thirst for this knowledge was unquenchable. Her sifting and her dredging of it had become an all-consuming obsession.

Each evening she would lie on her bed, a notebook open on her pillow and a pencil in her hand, writing detailed notes of everything Keith could tell her about his day. After he had gone, either to bed or downstairs to watch television with their mother, Maddie would work long hours into the night, examining vast wall charts drawn in crayon on the backs of curling lengths of the wallpaper she had found rolled up in a cardboard box in the kitchen. She would add and subtract information, pinning on scraps of paper in mounting columns, with headings scrawled on them and cross-references to pages in her notebooks. Spidery, penciled-in question marks peppered the surface of these charts that covered all the walls of her room.

Her notebooks were stacked along the floor, up against the wall, their spines labeled with colored stickers, reference numbers drawn underneath in a felt-tipped pen. In her need to root out the truth about the library, to lay all its secrets bare, Maddie was creating a library of her own.

She did not know for certain what she was looking for. But the more she discovered about the Tower Library, the more she felt convinced that the internationally respected institution was not what it seemed. The library was the cold stone heart of the town, pumping some unknown fear into the streets. She also knew that somewhere in the twisting tunnels of information, in that maze of her own making in which she was lost, somewhere there she would find Lexeter.

Meanwhile, outside her window, April blossomed into May. Birds taught their young to fly from nests in the overgrown gutters of the post office. The building now had its windows and doorways sealed by cement blocks. There were signs, fixed to the outside walls at three-foot intervals that read: KEEP OUT! DANGER OF DEATH! Each evening Maddie would see Keith glance at the building with a visible shudder as he crossed the road and hurried up the front path to the house, coming home from the library.

Maddie knew Keith's library timetable, so was able to prepare in advance for his homecoming and the frenzy of note-taking that followed. On Mondays he studied filing systems and worked on the transferring of files from one empty office to another, under the cold eye of Miss

Pring. Maddie made her notes in the notebook with the blue label. On Tuesdays he repaired damaged books using tape and glue. Maddie used her yellow-labeled notebook. On Wednesday it was ground-floor maintenance inspection with Potts, trudging from room to empty room, oiling door hinges and wrapping leaky pipes with cloth and insulating tape. Maddie used a gray-labeled book. On Thursday it was inter-library loans, filing requests for books from other libraries and sealing envelopes for sending out requests from the Tower Library. Maddie's notebook had a purple label. On Fridays Keith learned about different library cataloguing systems and helped with the shelving of books in the great Tower itself. Maddie used her notebook with the red label.

She had plenty of other notebooks. One for Potts (white label), one for Miss Pring (salmon pink label), and one for Lexeter. Lexeter's was a thick hardback notebook with a black-and-silver label. She also had a book for unexpected occurrences, like the time Keith was allowed to visit the second floor, creeping up the stairs with a tray of coffee cups for the deputy librarians, who were holding a meeting to discuss their coffee-break rotation in the Lesser Index Room. Keith had seen the index, or the lesser index, at any rate. The index was a record of every book that was housed in the library. The index was kept on cards, one for each book, the details typed onto the card, and all the cards filed away in a collection of huge dark cabinets containing drawer after drawer after drawer, all filled up with the Tower Library index cards.

She also kept a notebook for unsolved library mysteries. This book contained the torn fragment of a page of library shorthand taped to the inside cover, along with several pages of unsuccessful attempts to decode it. Then there was a collection of curious newspaper reports that Maddie recalled from the pages of the *Pridebridge Exchange*. She had jotted them down from memory. One was a report on a missing party of librarians from the famous Pridebridge Tower who had been lost in an ill-fated attempt to become the first team of public sector employees to swim across the twisting Pridebridge River. According to the report, they had made the attempt at night, without any accompanying vessel. No bodies were ever found. There were other reported disappearances too, which Maddie had recorded. The police chief's daughter and a reporter from the *Exchange* itself–both had vanished without a trace, having last been seen in the vicinity of the Tower Library.

It was also in this book that the details of the prisoner in the basement were written up. Maddie often turned to this notebook, flicking through its pages, many of which were still frustratingly blank. No matter how hard she begged or wheedled or bullied, she had not managed to persuade Keith to make another visit to the corridor with the cell door at the end of it.

One evening, waiting for Keith to get home, Maddie knelt to return the mysteries notebook to its place under the window and caught sight of Park standing under the lamppost outside the bricked-up post office with its "Danger of Death" signs. There had been no trace of Park since the accident inside the old building. Now he was back. He was not looking up at Maddie's window. He was not calling out. He was not singing. He had no audience, no cronies to impress. He was alone and he was silent. And he was obviously waiting for someone.

Park stiffened suddenly and stared down the road, his body rigid. Maddie squashed her face up against the windowpane, her cheek spread out on the cold glass. This way she was able to follow the direction of Park's gaze and to see what he was looking at. It was Keith, walking toward the house with his quick footsteps and his skinny legs, his satchel bumping against his chest.

Park had tensed like a vicious dog that had spied a rival. Maddie saw Keith falter in his step momentarily. He crossed the road. Park crossed too, moving purposefully to intercept his quarry.

Keith stopped. He glanced up and down the road.

Park bore down on him. Keith flinched. This was a different Park than the cruel bully who had taunted Maddie from down in the street on so many evenings. Park was alone now—his followers had deserted him after his cowardice in the post office incident. And he clearly blamed Keith for his fall from grace. Maddie could see it all in the tense set of his shoulders as he moved in on her brother. If his beatings had been bad before, they would be far worse now. There was a look of pitiless anger in his relentless stride. When he got to within a few feet of Keith, who was watching Park's approach as if mesmerized, he bent down and picked something up from the pavement. Park raised his arm. There was half a brick clutched in his fist.

Keith ran. He shot past Park, sprinting out across the road, running at a crouch. Park gave a wordless shout and turned. He went after Keith, the brick in his fist.

Maddie pulled her face from the windowpane. An outline in the shape of her flattened cheek was left printed in condensation on the glass. She spun around on her toes and ran, her footsteps quick and sure, out of her room and down the stairs and along the hall and up to the front door. Her hand gripped the doorknob, which turned in her sweaty palm. Then the door was open and she was outside in the street.

Chapter 11

It was like diving into the sea. A cold, clear sea. But she had no time to think about it. She was there to rescue her brother, who was facing Park somewhere outside. Park, mad and holding a broken brick.

Maddie crossed the road, the summer breeze flowing all about her like the pull of the tide. There was Keith. He was lying on his back on the ground, his head next to the base of the lamppost. His eyes were closed, his hands raised in front of his face, shaking, anticipating the blow to come. Park was standing over him. He looked as if he had lost all self-control. His face was red. There were tears of anger brimming in his eyes. His angelic features were contorted with rage. Snot bubbled in one nostril. He had raised the brick high in the air and was looking down at Keith, who was helpless and flinching on the ground. Park was going to hurt him very badly indeed.

Maddie swam toward them, her thoughts numb, her actions automatic. Her shadow, a great sprawling cloak of shade, fell over the two youths.

Park looked up. Mad Maddie Palmer stood before him.

Maddie read the emotions in his face as they bled from anger into astonishment and on into disgust and fear. His face whitened. She stared into his big, blue, bully boy's eyes. She saw herself reflected there, not as she really was, but as Park saw her: a huge grotesque maniac, a staring, mindless monster. She felt a phlegmy chuckle burble up in her throat and let a slow, moronic leer spread itself across her face. With what she hoped was a convincingly monstrous gait, Maddie shuffled forward. She gave another chuckle and raised a trembling hand toward Park, who had been standing transfixed, a look of dread on his face.

"No!" he said. "Don't touch me! Keep away!"

Maddie let out a sudden moaning cry and lunged toward him. Park screamed and leaped backward into the road. The blare of a truck's horn ripped into the summer air. Maddie had not even been aware of its thunderous approach. Now she stood staring, her jaw slack with genuine bewilderment, as the huge vehicle bore down on Park, who stood in the road with the brick still raised in his fist.

What happened next Maddie could never really understand. Park himself probably could not explain what he did. The surge of violence and fear-charged adrenaline that had taken hold of him proved too much for his self-control. He threw the brick with all the force he could muster, straight through the windshield of the oncoming vehicle.

The truck careened across the road, its tires screaming and great clouds of black fumes belching out of its exhaust pipe. It mounted the pavement and its trailer swung around, plowing into the front of the post office.

There was a brief moment of stillness. Then, coughing and spluttering, the driver jumped from the cabin. He stared wildly about, brushing broken pieces of glass from the shattered windshield from his clothing. A cut on his forehead oozed dark blood.

"I . . . I . . . I might have been killed!" he stammered, his eyes wide. "You!" He caught sight of Park, standing close to the curb. "You! You tried to kill me! You threw a brick at my truck, you little—Hey! Come back here!"

Park had started to run.

"I don't believe this," the truck driver yelled. "I just

don't believe this!" He set out after Park at a determined jog. "I'm gonna get you!" he bellowed down the road. "You see if I don't! And when I've finished with you, the police will get you! The police, d'you hear me?"

Maddie watched all this, still standing by the lamp-post. Keith was sitting at her feet. The rear of the truck had seemed certain to crush them, but it had swung harmlessly by, doing no more than ruffling their hair in a cloud of choking fumes.

Keith coughed, his shoulders heaving, and then he shuddered.

"He was going to smash my face in with that brick," he said quietly, his eyes on the ground. He looked up at his sister.

"Maddie," he said, wrinkling his brow, the tone of his voice changing. "Maddie, you're outside! You came out of the house!"

Maddie slowly turned her head, gazing across the road at the outside of the house, at the lamppost she had watched so often, the tire marks in the road, and the truck leaning unevenly on its broken tires, surrounded by the debris of the post office's front wall. Then she looked down at Keith. As if from a great distance, she heard him yell and saw him roll quickly out of the way before her vision clouded into darkness. Her legs folded under her and she collapsed onto the ground in a dead faint.

Chapter 12

Maddie opened her eyes and there was the sky. It spread out before her and around her. It filled her vision. Great crumpled mountains of cloud were moving with the slow, unstoppable grace of Alpine glaciers. Beyond them, strips of gauzy vapor were stippled across a pale blue expanse. Through the gaps in the clouds, the open sky deepened to an endless, shimmering turquoise.

Maddie gazed into forever and a smile broke across her face. Her memory was not so formidable after all, she realized. Somewhere during her years inside, she had forgotten the sky. Not what it looked like, but what it felt like.

And then, drifting across her mind, there came another misplaced memory. An image of Grandad Lemon at her side, towering above her, dressed in an old woolen coat. They were walking across the rough grass of Pridebridge Common, back from feeding the ducks on the pond.

"Wow! Look at that sky!" he had said, and Maddie looked up from watching her feet in the grass and saw the sky painted over with a glowing winter sunset that made her gasp, it was so beautiful. As they stood watching, a flight of wild geese passed over, black against the sky, their wings swishing, uttering a few mournful honks as they disappeared beyond the tree line.

Something was intruding into these memories. Maddie became aware of two faces, both with identical expressions—brows anxiously puckered, mouths pursed— peering down at her. Mrs. Palmer and Keith were bending over her. She was lying on her back on the pavement.

"Maddie?" Mrs. Palmer leaned forward and prodded her daughter in the stomach with a bony finger. "Maddie, are you . . . mmm, yes . . . all right?"

"He loved the sky, didn't he, Mom?" Maddie said, smiling.

Mrs. Palmer wrinkled her nose. "Keithy, what's she talking about?" she asked.

Keith leaned forward. "Maddie, you're not hurt are you?" he said. "I mean ... you can stand up and everything, can't you?"

"Oh, I should think so," Maddie said, "but it's very comfortable here on the pavement. And there's such a wonderful view!"

Keith bobbed his head and chewed his lower lip.

"Maddie, the police will be here any minute to start clearing up the crash. I think we should go back into the house. You know, it might be simpler if they didn't find us here."

"Go back, in the house? Why should I want to do that?" Maddie spread out her arms and yawned cavernously. "Still, now that I think about it, perhaps a light snack might be in order."

She rolled herself onto her knees and stood up unsteadily. She limped to the curb with Keith and Mrs. Palmer on either side of her, their shoulders hunched, their hands clasped anxiously in front of them. Lying in the gutter was a large stone slab that had been torn off the front of the post office building when the truck had crashed into it. Maddie looked at it. Carved into the stone was an inscription:

This stone was laid by
Councilman Silas Lemon.

"Silas Lemon? Wasn't that Grandad's name?" Maddie said.

"Yes, Maddie, yes, yes," said her mother. "Ooh, he was a rare one, my dad was. He was a real man of the people. He laid that stone fifty years ago, when he was on the council, before I was even born, mmm, yes. It was to mark the opening of the brand-new post office. Oh, and look at it now! Ruined!"

"I didn't know he was a councilman," Maddie said when she and Keith were sitting around the kitchen table. Mrs. Palmer was squatting over the four-slice toaster, down on the floor by the wall socket, waiting for the toast to pop up.

"Yes, but they threw him out, didn't they!" she said. "Too honest, he was. Mmm, yes. Wouldn't take bribes!"

Mrs. Palmer shook her head. "Now, that's enough ancient history for one day!" she said, clapping her hands together. "What about you, Maddie, going outside for the first time in I don't know how long! Ooh, I do hope you've broken that stay at home habit! I mean, I didn't want to argue with you, 'cause you know how you can throw a tantrum when you don't get your own way, but really! Never leaving the house at all, for years and years! D'you know? I was starting to worry!"

Keith tried to suppress a sudden snort of laughter. There was an edge of panic to his hissing giggle and shaking shoulders. Maddie could tell he was as close to tears as he was to laughter. It was no surprise, considering what they had just been through. What *did* surprise Maddie was that she felt so calm herself. Not only had she faced Keith's traumas with him, she had also left the shelter of the house for the first time in thirteen years. And yet she felt calm. Too calm. The sensation of moving, acting, thinking automatically, that she had had when she ran out into the street to confront Park, had returned. She felt numb.

The first signs that this emotional numbness was starting to wear off hit her just after she finished her fifth piece of toast, washed down with her third mug of cocoa. Her stomach was suddenly gripped by inner turmoil. It was like an underwater volcano erupting inside her.

She sat very still and gripped the tabletop. Beads of sweat broke out across her forehead.

"Maddie," said Mrs. Palmer, "you look a bit green around the gills. Is everything all right?"

Maddie jumped to her feet and bolted for the door. She pounded upstairs to the bathroom and got there just in time to be violently sick into the toilet bowl. She sat down on the floor, coughing and moaning under her breath. She blew her nose on a length of toilet paper. Keith appeared at the door, eyes wide, holding out a glass of water.

"Keith!" she gasped. "What's going on, Keith? I'm never sick! What a waste of toast!"

Keith stared at her, big-eyed and silent. She pulled the glass of water out of his hand and took a couple of sips.

"I think . . ." she said slowly. "I think I need some air."

Maddie spent the next eight hours outside in the back garden. It was not a very large garden. In fact, not having been in it since the age of two, she was amazed at how tiny it now seemed. With the sky above her, and the grass beneath her feet, she paced up and down while twilight drained into purple night.

By midnight the sky was dusted with stars. Maddie walked up and down the garden. The monotonous swish of her feet through the tangled grass was the only sound, apart from the distant noise of night traffic. Every now and then she would glance at the house. She was thinking of her room, the wall charts and notebooks. She knew them so well, she did not need to have them in front of her to use them. In her mind she sifted once more through the reservoir of information she had created. At the same time she sought another connection. Why had she not felt able to leave the house until now? What had so terrified her as a two-year-old that she had buried the memory where she could not find it, and locked herself away from the sky for so long? The answer, she was now convinced, lay in the echoing corridors of the Tower Library. In the morning she would go there and find out the truth at last.

Chapter 13

Maddie began to get cold soon after one o'clock in the morning. She brought out a striped blanket, which she wrapped around her body, and a dusty, moth-eaten old coat of her mother's that she threw over her shoulders like a cape.

Keith and Mrs. Palmer were asleep. The house was in darkness. The pine trees in the garden next door were black against the sky. They bowed and shivered in the night breeze. Maddie glanced at them, unseeing. In her mind the dark puzzle of the Tower Library had begun to shift and flow and take shape. A light of understanding flickered on.

By four o'clock the sky had lightened to a dreamy rose petal pink and Maddie had grown tired of waiting for her mother to wake up. There was something she wanted to ask her. She threw open the back door and barged through the kitchen, the trailing blanket catching on the towering piles of boxes and containers. She clumped up the stairs, not bothering to keep quiet. She was wide awake, more awake than she had felt in years. Sleep, either for herself or anyone else, was now a very low priority.

She walked into her mother's room and over to the bed. She looked down at Mrs. Palmer, who lay on her back, her hands clutching the blanket. Her head was tipped back. Her eyelids twitched and flicked. She was muttering in her sleep.

"Butter . . . mmm, yes . . . best butter . . . none of your . . . mmm, yes . . . marge . . . My Maddie's coming out shopping with me this afternoon, ladies . . . So proud . . . Butter! Mmm . . . yes."

"Mom!" Maddie said, her voice loud in the gloomy bedroom. The heavy woolen curtains blocked out the light of dawn.

Mrs. Palmer opened her eyes.

"Oh, my word! I was dreaming I was in a submarine again!" she said.

Maddie ignored this.

"Mom. There's something I have to ask you about."

"Maddie?" Her mother's voice was croaky. Old sounding. "Maddie? What time is it? And what's that you've got on?"

"I was cold. Now look, I didn't wake you up to get early-morning fashion advice! I want you to tell me something. It's important. You're not going to like it, but you've got to tell me. Now is the time when we all have to face up to our fears. It's now or never. So. Tell me why you're afraid of closets!"

"Ooh, now, Maddie." Mrs. Palmer pulled the blanket tighter up around her neck. "I'm not . . . mmm, yes . . . *frightened* of them exactly . . ."

"Mom, you *are* frightened of closets. . . . Now tell me why!"

"It's . . . it's . . . a bit silly, really. You don't want to hear my old stories, now . . ."

"Tell me!"

"All right, all right, Maddie. I'll tell you. It's because of the time I heard one talk."

"Heard what talk?"

"A closet—well, more of a wardrobe really, Maddie. I heard a wardrobe talk. Mmm. Yes. It scared me, I can tell you."

"I should think it did, Mom. And when did this happen?"

"It was the night your grandad disappeared. I'd gone to his apartment . . . I don't suppose you remember his apartment . . ."

"Of course I do! It had pictures of birds or something hanging on the wall, and a big cabinet full of china . . . I remember it."

"So you do. Well, anyway, I was just going there to see how he was and to thank him for taking you to the library, because, you know, in those days the Tower Library used to be a real lending library where anyone could go to borrow a book, not just high-blown old professors and the like—"

"I know, I know! Tell me about the wardrobe!"

"Well, there were these two fellers lugging a wardrobe down the steps of Grandad's apartment. I asked them what they were doing and they said they'd been given the wrong delivery address and were taking the wardrobe back to the depot. And that's when it spoke to me."

"Really. And what did it say?"

"It said, 'Don't listen to them, they're lying!' Something like that, hard to tell, its voice was sort of muffled. I jumped out of my skin . . . mmm, yes . . . And I said, 'Did you hear that?' but the delivery men didn't know what I was talking about. I was hearing voices! I tell you, Maddie, it scared me so. The wardrobe kept yelling at me, but I put my hands over my ears. I didn't want to end up like my uncle Ned, you see . . . mmm, yes . . . He used to hear voices talking to him through the mailbox. One day they found him floating in the river, dead as mutton, and not a stitch of clothing on him!"

"And what about Grandad? Did you tell him about the wardrobe?"

"Well, no. He was gone. Disappeared. No one ever saw him again."

"I see," said Maddie. She turned and walked out of the room, the blanket trailing along the floor behind her. She heard her mother calling after her.

"Ooh, Maddie! Why did you go and remind me of that, eh? It's got me all jittery thinking about talking wardrobes. If I end up stark naked in the river, it'll be all your fault!"

Maddie walked into Keith's room. He was already awake, sitting on the edge of the bed, pulling on a pair of socks.

"Come out for a walk, Maddie," he said. "I want to show you something."

It wasn't far. The dawn streets were awash with silver light. They walked around the corner and they were there. Lemon House. It had been built twelve years earlier. Maddie had never seen the building. It was not very tall, only five stories. Even so, she was breathless and sweating by the time they had climbed the stairs to the top-floor landing. The elevator was broken down, a handwritten "Out of Order" notice stuck to the doors with a piece of tape.

Maddie leaned forward, her hands clasping her knees, and gave vent to a rasping cough.

"One flight of stairs I can handle," she said croakily, "but five! That's ridiculous! Who lives up here, a family of Olympic athletes? Perhaps I should go on a diet. Depressing thought . . ."

Keith was standing by the window.

"I come up here sometimes," he said. "The view . . ." His voice trailed off. Maddie looked out through the grimy window over Pridebridge. The town sparkled in the light of a new day. The sun was burning white in the clear blue sky. Martins whirled like tiny black boomerangs over the rooftops on the road where Grandad Lemon had once lived. Sunlight, broken into a thousand glistening stars, bounced off the river that curved through the grassy common. And beyond the river, standing gaunt and tall against the summer sky, looking down over the houses and shops and factories, was the Tower Library.

"It's a beautiful day, Keith," said Maddie. She sighed long and deep, still gazing out over the rooftops.

"All right!" She shook herself and turned away. "It's time we were going."

"We? Us? Going where?" Keith's eyebrows knitted and he bit his lower lip.

"There!" said Maddie, and she swung back to the window and stabbed one thick finger in the direction of the library. "Today, Keith," she said, her eyes blazing, "today we take the Tower!"

Chapter 14

"Go on then," said Maddie.

Keith tapped in the code sequence on the security buzzer. He listened for the mechanical response, a sound like a wasp trapped in a jam jar, and then pulled open the library side door. Potts was standing there, just inside the entrance, blocking the corridor, arms folded across his chest.

Keith went rigid. Maddie cleared her throat and stepped forward.

"Good morning, Mr. Potts," she said, smiling. "Keith asked me if I would like to accompany him today. I am fascinated by the Tower Library and am so looking forward to helping my brother with all his duties."

Maddie tried to walk past Potts, but the big security man blocked her way.

"People try all sorts of things to get in here, all sorts of things," he said. "Let me give you a for instance. There was a feller once, claimed he was a bigwig from some northern university, tried to bluff his way in. I played along for a while. Gave him directions. Down to the basement. He left here in a hurry, as I recall. White in the face and screaming blue murder. We never saw *him* again." He let out a mirthless chuckle.

"That's all very interesting, Mr. Potts," said Maddie, "but if you'd just move aside, I believe it's nearly time for Keith and me to start work."

Potts leaned forward and shoved his big red face up close to Maddie's.

"No one gets in here without the proper authority," he said. "No one! So you can get out. Now!"

Potts took hold of the door and pushed it. Maddie was shoved back outside. She saw Keith, whom Potts had hustled inside, shake his head, his forehead wrinkled. Then the door closed and she was alone.

She gave a shrug and walked slowly back to the road, thinking of the last time she had been to the library, thirteen years ago with Grandad Lemon. There had been a few shops opposite the public library entrance. Now that the library was no longer open to the public, all of the shops but one were shut down, their windows boarded, the doors padlocked or nailed shut. The one remaining shop sold used car tires. The heavy black tires were stacked up in columns on the pavement, rising up all around the shop front. A narrow path, flanked by eight-foot-high tire columns, led to the open door. Maddie stood in the doorway. She could see a crude wooden counter and a man wearing heavily stained overalls leaning against it. A second man lounged behind the counter. They occupied the only space available in the tiny shop. The rest was given over to more rows of tires, stacked in dusty black pillars, reaching up to the ceiling. A naked bulb hanging from a low iron girder was the only source of light.

Maddie stepped inside. The two men stared at her.

"Hello," she said. The men continued to stare. Both of them were chewing gum, letting out a quiet, rhythmic squelching.

"This used to be a baker's shop, a long time ago," said Maddie. "I remember my grandad buying me some cake. I don't suppose you've got any food I could have, do you?"

The two men looked at each other.

"You see, I missed breakfast this morning and I'm beginning to feel hungry. No? Well, never mind."

One of the men cleared his throat.

"Used tires," he grunted.

"What?" said Maddie. "Have I used tires? No, actually, I haven't. I tell you what, though," Maddie added, reaching a hand toward a book of matches that lay on the counter next to a packet of cigarettes, "I think I could probably use these, if that's all right."

She swept up the matches and backed out of the shop.

"I'll bring them back later. Thank you!" she called, waving a hand as she walked out past the piled up tires. The two men sat, unmoving, staring after her in silence. They had stopped chewing. Both their mouths hung open.

Maddie headed back toward the library. She glanced at her watch. It was another hour to go before Potts went for his break. She knew all the routines of the library and its staff by heart. At ten o'clock Potts would be in the ground-floor staff room leafing through a copy of the *Pridebridge Exchange.* Getting inside the library then would just be a matter of tapping in the security code, which she had also learned by heart, and letting herself in by the side door.

She walked around the library building, squinting up at its featureless brickwork, and shrugging her shoulders against the unexpected chill as she passed under the shadow of the tower itself.

Four times all the way around took her up to ten o'clock. By that time the clear blue sky had been covered over with heavy gray clouds. The clouds built up steadily until they blotted out the sun. Maddie shivered.

"Looks like a good time to be going inside," she said, and headed for the side door.

She gained entry unchallenged. An empty corridor stretched ahead of her. The door marked SECURITY was there at her shoulder, just as Keith had described it so many times. She tried the door. It opened. Maddie grinned.

"Careless, Mr. Potts, very careless!" she said aloud.

Through the door was a small office. A bank of video surveillance monitors, all switched off, covered one wall. There was a desk and a swivel chair. The black plastic upholstery on the chair was split, the off-white stuffing bulging out. On the wall behind the desk was a board to which a row of small brass hooks had been attached. Keys hung from the hooks. Beneath each hook was a room number.

"Very careless indeed, Mr. Potts!" Maddie said. "But, then again, we mustn't forget your dreadful memory for figures."

The room numbers were not based on any logical code or sequence. But Maddie knew which rooms they represented. Keith had noted them all down for her. He had drawn maps and described his daily circuits around the empty corridors.

But one key was hanging above an unfamiliar number. The number was B13. This was the key she took. All the other rooms she knew to be empty offices or storerooms or the personnel office where Miss Pring would be seated, headphones on and dictaphone working, scribbling shorthand. They were of no interest to her. But room B13? Now where could that be?

Maddie followed the route that Keith had taken the very first time he had come to the library, when he had been trying to find the personnel office. She came to the stairs leading down to the basement. Standing on the top step, she strained her ears for any sound of footsteps or voices. The pipes in the wall were humming. The building creaked and sighed. She heard a distant rumble of thunder from outside.

Maddie swallowed. She could feel her heart beating, pushing the blood through her veins. She thought of her dream. The eye pressed to the spy hole. She thought of Keith, hearing the thumping on the locked door and the anguished cries of the prisoner. She shook her head and tucked loose strands of her hair behind her ears.

"Now," she whispered to herself, "let's have a look down here."

Slowly, one step at a time, Maddie descended the staircase.

Chapter 15

In the basement corridor the humming of the water pipes was louder than ever, throbbing in Maddie's ears like the pulsing of the blood in her veins. There was the cell door, with its spy hole, down at the end of the corridor. Maddie glanced at the unmarked door to her left. It was heavy and paneled and made of dark stained wood. Beneath the tarnished brass handle was a keyhole.

Maddie blinked. The key from Potts's office was hot in her sweaty palm. Impulsively, she slipped it into the keyhole. The lock turned smoothly. The door swung open. Inside was total darkness. So this was room B13.

It had to be. This was the only part of the building that Keith had not mapped out for her. B13 was the only room number he had not noted down.

She ran her hand up and down the smooth cold plaster of the wall, just inside the door. Her fingertips felt the familiar form of a light switch. She flipped it and strip lights blinked into life, flickering for a second or two from light to dark, like lightning splitting a night sky. The light revealed an enormous room, its walls lined with filing cabinets. In the center of the room a number of these cabinets had been left standing in an untidy huddle. The room was still. Still and silent, but for the hum of the pipes.

Maddie approached the first of the filing cabinets and opened one of the drawers. It was stuffed with manila folders. She pulled one out and flipped it open. There were pages of notes in the familiar shorthand code that she had never been able to crack, and behind that, more pages, typewritten, not in code, on paper that bore the blue crest of the Pridebridge Police Force stamped in the top right-hand corner. These were records. Criminal records. Crimes solved and unsolved.

Maddie dropped the folder on the floor and moved on, opening drawers at random, glancing at the files they contained. Police records, medical records, council records, school records; they were all here, every detail of life in Pridebridge.

She moved into the center of the room, where the spare cabinets had been left. Looking at them again, there did seem to be some kind of order to the way they had been placed. They stood in a rough circle, like the standing stones of Stonehenge, but with extra cabinets filling up the inside of the temple.

And then she saw it. On the polished wooden floor, a map had been painted. It was a plan of Pridebridge. Here was the river, snaking past the towering cabinets, stretching all the way across town. There was a bare space that represented the common. The outline of the lake had been painted blue. And there were the roads, painted gray. It was on the roads that the cabinets had been placed. Each cabinet corresponded to a different road or group of roads. The cabinets had rows of postcard-sized drawers in them. Maddie reached out and pulled open a drawer. It was filled with index cards, each bearing a name. Here, carefully filed in alphabetical order and arranged according to the streets in which they lived and worked, was a record of the entire population of the town.

"Impressive, isn't it?" The voice cracked harshly through the stillness of the room. Maddie spun around. She already knew who was there. The voice was enough. It was Lexeter.

"I see you are admiring my Greater Index Room, where all the crimes, the secrets, the fears of all the people are stored, ready for me to use whenever I need. You'd be surprised what some people want to keep hidden. With the information in this room I can persuade them to do anything I say. Otherwise, one word from me and they could find themselves losing their job, or their home, or facing a lengthy prison sentence.

"Of course, there are some poor souls who have no secrets. They are the bleating, mindless sheep of Pridebridge, who question nothing, think nothing, and do nothing. There's quite a flock of them. Your mother, for instance, is one."

"My mother?" Maddie clenched her fists and glared at the figure in the doorway. "You leave my mother alone."

He stood there, tall and gaunt in his gray coat. His head was bowed, permanently stooped from years of hunching over the drawers of filing cabinets. The skin on his face was shiny in the yellow electric light.

"Oh, don't worry about your precious mother," he sneered. "Sheep are no threat to me! All this," he said, nodding at his filing cabinets, "made sure of that. There are others, a few, that I've had to deal with more harshly, as you will see, Maddie Palmer." His voice was thoughtful, with an undercurrent of menace.

As he walked toward her, Maddie felt a cold sweat break out all over her body.

She could not move her feet. A terrible fear was turning her blood to ice. She felt a strange, empty sensation at the back of her head.

And then she remembered. At last she remembered. Thirteen years ago. Her final trip to the public library. The scene began to unfold in her memory, all the sights and the sounds intact, as fresh as if it were happening to her now.

She was two years old. She was leafing through a book. There were pictures of nasty-looking pixies dancing around tree trunks and spring-cleaning their toadstool houses. She dropped the book on the floor and looked for Grandad Lemon. He was talking to a tall man in a gray coat. A man who was stooped at the neck. They had headed away from her, down the aisle between the shelves, leaving the children's book section behind. Grandad Lemon had forgotten her.

Maddie followed Grandad, but she went down the wrong aisle. She could hear him on the other side of the bookshelves. He was angry with the stooped man. The two men were talking in fierce whispers.

"You think you can scare this whole town into silence?" Grandad Lemon said. "Well, you can't scare me!"

"Some people are too stubborn to realize when they've lost," said the voice of the other man, "and too stupid to realize when they'd be best off leaving well enough alone!"

"You think you can just take this town and turn it into your own private estate, like some medieval baron?"

"Yes, ex-Councilman Lemon, that is precisely what I do think. In fact, it's happened already. The chief of police, the director of the health department, the chief executive of the town council, they will all go along with anything I decide, because they are all too gutless to risk having their careers ruined!"

Maddie wanted to find Grandad Lemon, to drag him away from this horrible man with his sneering voice and his shiny face. She walked to the end of the aisle and peered around the end of the bookshelf. Grandad was there with his back to her. The shiny-faced man looked over his shoulder and into her eyes.

"And if anyone ever dares to step out of line," he continued, speaking to Grandad, "I shall just have to remind them of what happened to you, won't I?"

"What are you talking about? Is that a threat?" Grandad Lemon blustered.

"Oh, no, not a threat." The man in the gray coat was still looking at Maddie, but Grandad had not noticed her. "Not a threat. It's a promise."

"Well, you can't scare me!" Grandad said. "I'm taking my granddaughter home and I'm not setting foot in your stinking library ever again!"

"Actually, I'm suspending the public lending library

service until further notice. As of tonight. But I expect I shall be seeing you soon, ex-Councilman Lemon. Good night!"

Maddie stared up in dismay at Grandad's retreating back as he hurried to where he thought he had left her, back in the children's book section. She was alone with the ghastly face of the head librarian staring down at her. He took two steps forward and stood, towering above her.

"If you understood anything of what you've just overheard, little girl, then, if I were you, I would forget it."

Maddie stared up at him, craning her neck. He towered above her, his eyes boring down into hers. His words, "forget it . . . forget it," were echoing around her head, burning into her mind. She mustered her resentment and stuck her lower lip out.

"Won't forget," she muttered in sullen defiance. She really did not like this man. She wanted to run away, but she could not think how to get past him and back to her grandad. She fought a sudden urge to cry. Her defiance was ebbing fast.

"Won't forget?" said Lexeter in his fierce whisper. "Well, I think it's about time you started!" He rocked back on his heels. "I don't want to see you again," he went on, his voice loaded with menace. "I don't want to hear about you again. I don't want to think about you again. Not ever. You go home and stay there. Forget all about this little conversation of ours. Otherwise . . ." And here he drew the forefinger of one hand across his throat, slowly, and with a rasping scrape of fingernail on skin.

"Bad things, little girl," he said, "very bad things!"

Maddie shook herself out of the past with a twitch of her shoulders. She pushed stray hair back behind her ears and forced herself to look at Lexeter, still tall and stooped and dressed in a gray coat, walking toward her through the Greater Index Room.

"In my dream," Maddie said, her voice no more than a whisper, "in my dream you were very tall. Tall like a tower." She swallowed and her voice gained in strength. "You were tall, but you were unstable. Very frightening looking, swaying backward and forward against the sky. But when you fell, you smashed to bits, as if you were made out of glass."

Lexeter stopped.

"What are you babbling about, girl? Your mind has obviously gone soft. I knew that doctor was a fool to worry, and I told him as much when he made his report."

He curled his shiny pink top lip into a sneer. "So this is it, is it? The great Pridebridge uprising! After thirteen years I am faced with putting down a rebellion by ex-Councilman Lemon's two half-witted grandchildren."

"Keith's got nothing to do with this," said Maddie.

Lexeter gave a mirthless laugh.

"Don't be ridiculous," he said. "He's up to his neck in it. But I'll make him sorry! If you were to look in the filing cabinet to your left, filed under Palmer, K., you will discover that I have quite enough evidence against your Keith to send him away to an institution for young offenders. His part in those unfortunate incidents at the old post office can be made to sound very dark indeed, in the hands of the right lawyer. But don't worry. He won't be lonely in the institution. Park is already there. I expect I can arrange for them to share a cell!"

Lexeter sniffed and stepped forward. He was unpleasantly close now. Maddie tried not to breathe in the suffocating odor that rose from his coat, a smell like the dusty, stale air of windowless rooms and mildewed, unread books rotting on the shelf.

The head librarian glanced to his left at the nearest filing cabinet. A small, pale gray spider was crawling across the top of one of the drawers. Lexeter brought his hand down hard, crushing the spider beneath his palm. He fixed Maddie with an unblinking stare.

"I shall destroy your pitiful uprising, crush it, just as I

crushed this wretched crawling thing. You're going to wish you'd stayed at home, Maddie Palmer." Lexeter leaned forward and sneered at her, revealing a jagged row of long yellow teeth.

Chapter 16

"You . . . !" Maddie took a step toward the head librarian. Her fear melted away, leaving a molten core of anger and contempt. Lexeter was no longer a dark, stooping giant, a nightmarish childhood monster too frightening to even think about. Here he stood, a shriveled old man who enjoyed frightening little children and killing spiders. He was pathetic.

He spoke, but now his voice sounded frail and whining rather than chilling and sinister.

"I do have a problem with you," he said. "Since you've not been out and about much, I've got nothing filed under Palmer, M. But no matter. Your grandfather disappeared. I don't see why you can't too."

He took a mobile phone out of his coat pocket and pressed in a few numbers.

"Potts!" he said into the phone. "Get down here now. Bring the cell key. We have a new acquisition to file in our local history archive."

Everything happened very quickly. Potts arrived with his keys jiggling in his hand and an expression that was both cruel and smug smeared across his face. Maddie was marched out of the room and along the basement corridor. Potts pulled back the grate on the spy hole in the cell door. He peered in, then grunted. The key was turned in the lock. Maddie was shoved into the cell and the door was slammed behind her. The lock moved with a harsh metallic squeal and echoing footsteps receded into the distance.

Maddie stood in the harsh light from the single unshaded bulb that hung from the ceiling. She stood and stared at the man sitting on the edge of the bed. This was the owner of the voice behind the door. This was the prisoner of the Tower Library.

He was an old man, very scrawny and wearing a filthy vest. His long, sinewy arms were bare. They were streaked with reddish dust and dried mud.

"I knew it," he said, his voice cracked, not just with age, but also with emotion. "I knew someone would come. I knew, in the end, someone would have the nerve to take a risk."

His face was lost within a wild shock of white hair and a thistledown beard. Only his eyes were visible, like shiny black coals, smiling out at her. And it was the eyes that held her. And looking into those eyes, Maddie realized who this old man was.

"Grandad?" she said. "Grandad Lemon?"

The old man gasped and jumped to his feet.

"It can't be! Maddie Palmer? My own granddaughter! My own kith and kin? Why, when I think of all the nights I've lain on this bed, sobbing my old heart out, or knelt on that floor, bashing my old head against that door, shouting 'Nooo!' because I'd lost hope of ever finding a single person to face up to Lexeter and his wretched library of lost souls. And all along, all along, it was you! You, Maddie Palmer, coming to spring me from my prison cell and burn down the library!"

"Well, yes, I suppose you're right," said Maddie. "It is me. And, actually, I did bring some matches. I sort of guessed there might be records in here that were being misused and might need getting rid of. So I borrowed some."

Maddie pulled out the matches from her pocket, grinning at Grandad Lemon, who grinned back. They stood there, looking at each other for a moment before bursting into peals of laughter. Maddie flung her huge arms around her grandad's bony shoulders. The old man grabbed her face in his hands and began leaping up and down in a wild, celebratory dance.

"Argh! Mind my neck!" Maddie shouted through her laughter. Grandad let her go and spun himself around on one foot, whirling faster and faster and then suddenly stopping, arms outstretched.

"Olé!" he bellowed.

"Now," he said, draping one muddy arm around Maddie's neck. "Now we make our move. Now, while he thinks he's got us beat."

"Grandad," said Maddie, "quite apart from the fact that I have no idea how you came to be here or what happened to you thirteen years ago, I'm also wondering how you think we can make any kind of move when we're both locked in this cell."

"Simple," said Grandad Lemon. "I've built myself a tunnel!"

He bent down and grabbed hold of the worn rug that was spread out by the bed. He pulled it away with a magician's flourish, revealing a large stone, somewhat paler in color than the other floor-stones. He hooked his skinny fingers under the stone and heaved it out of position. There was a dark hole beneath it, leading straight down. Without another word he swung his legs over the lip of the hole and dropped out of sight into the blackness.

Maddie looked doubtfully at the hole. She leaned toward it and called down.

"Er, Grandad? Exactly how *wide* is this tunnel of yours?"

Chapter 17

Much to Maddie's relief, the tunnel turned out to be both wide and tall. It was more of a cavern than a tunnel, with a ceiling that stretched into darkness above her and sides far enough apart to allow her and Grandad Lemon to walk side by side.

"I normally find my way by touch," said Grandad Lemon, swinging the glowing lantern in one hand, setting the shadows dancing. "The last book of matches I managed to get hold of got used up five years ago. But since you were good enough to bring some, we can have light. So, what do you think of my tunnel?"

"It's . . . er, very nice," Maddie said, glancing around at the wood shoring up the tunnel's sides.

"Turned out quite lovely, if I do say so myself," said Grandad, slapping one of the wooden beams and un-loosing an avalanche of crumbling earth that cascaded down from the tunnel roof.

"I started digging twelve years ago," he went on. "I used a teaspoon at first. Later, when the tunnel led me to some basement storerooms, I got my hands on better tools. I got more ambitious. I worked on the height and the width. Most escape tunnels don't cater to the comfort of the tunnel user. But I like to see this as something of a five-star tunnel. Top notch, so to speak."

"But, if you dug this tunnel so long ago," said Maddie curiously, "why didn't you escape?"

"Ah! Well, now. That's a good question."

Grandad stopped and turned to face Maddie, the lamp in his hand casting a flickering light over his ancient white-haired head, setting his hair aglow, so that he looked like a fluffy white dandelion.

"You see, when Lexeter sent his heavies to get me that evening after I'd taken you home from the library, after they'd bundled me into that wardrobe they brought with them—clever trick—and after they'd taken me away, after your mom, *my own daughter,* had failed to recognize her father's voice and hadn't rescued me, well, after all that, when I was in my cell, down in the Tower Library basement, I did, I have to admit it, get a bit down in the mouth. I thought to myself, why bother to escape while no one in the whole town has the gumption to stand against Lexeter? I thought I'd wait until someone did. Even if no one came looking for *me*, then there were always the others."

"Others?" queried Maddie. "There are others?"

Grandad nodded. "I've got a pretty shrewd idea he's got a few more prisoners hidden away in this Tower Library somewhere. Still," he sighed, "no one came. So I started digging the tunnel, as a kind of hobby. A pastime, while I waited for someone else to join the battle. I wasn't the only one who knew what Lexeter was up to, with his files and his coded shorthand. But the others were either too scared of him, or they thought they could control him.

"In the end, he took control of *them,* of everything, of everyone. This so-called world famous library is just a front. It's a sham! A con! There hasn't been a genuine professor here for years. Don't believe what you read in the papers. The editor of the *Pridebridge Exchange* has got a particularly fat file with his name on it in the Greater Index Room. The truth is, Lexeter is a gangster, no more and no less. A gangster running a particularly nasty extortion racket.

"But he's a clever one, I'll grant him that. No computers. They're too easy to tap into, too open to the general public. He needs to keep things shrouded in mystery, to build up an atmosphere of fear. He lives off the fear of the people, see. He takes whatever he wants.

"But he hasn't gotten involved in murder, not yet, anyway. He knows just where to draw the line. Think about it. No one was that bothered when I disappeared. Glad to see the back of me, a lot of them. But a body would have forced them to act. So that's why he kept me locked up.

"Officially, I am the local history archive. They made me put down my childhood memories of life in old Pridebridge on tape. I told all about the famous boot dunking ritual, where the first Pridebridge man to be father of a baby born after February first each year has his boots thrown in the river. If they float, it's a sign that it's going to be a good year. I also reminisced about the zeppelin that got shot down and crashed on the common, burning for seven days and seven nights—"

"I've never heard any of these stories," Maddie interrupted.

"'Course not. I made them all up. You don't think I'd waste anything so precious as the truth on the likes of Lexeter, do you?"

They were walking again, tripping through the tunnels that twisted this way and that, muddling the senses in dusty darkness. As the tunnels coiled down in sloping curves, Maddie became aware that the floor was getting very slippery. As they continued, the floor became distinctly wet. Soon water was sloshing around their ankles.

"Sort of a drainage problem in this part of the tunnel," Grandad said. "It dates back to the time I accidentally dug through into an underground river. It never gets all that deep, though, not unless it's raining really hard."

Maddie remembered the thunderstorm that was raging in the outside world. But Grandad Lemon was still talking.

"It's hard to tell where you're going when you're digging. It's all hit and miss, really. That's another reason I never escaped through this tunnel. I never could find the way out."

Maddie stopped and stared at her grandad, cold river water swirling around her knees.

"So where does this tunnel lead?"

"Well, I know it seems nuts," Grandad said with a wry chuckle, "seeing as the tunnel took twelve years to dig and takes twenty minutes to walk along from end to end—but, apart from a couple of detours to some basement storerooms, the only place it leads to is the room next door to my cell."

"What!" said Maddie.

"Ah," said Grandad, "but that room is the Greater Index Room." He held up the matches that he had taken from Maddie to light the lamp with, and a wicked grin appeared through the floating tendrils of his beard.

Chapter 18

They entered the Greater Index Room up through the floor. The tunnel ended in a flight of crumbling stairs carved out of the red earth. Grandad Lemon scampered ahead, the lantern swinging wildly in his hand. Maddie stomped up the steps behind him.

"More stairs," she muttered under her breath. But Grandad did not hear her. He was standing on the top step pushing at the boards that roofed the tunnel. There was a splintering creak and the boards collapsed upward. The Greater Index Room, a vast cavern of inky darkness, stretched out around and above them.

Grandad scrambled up out of the tunnel. Maddie followed him at a more delicate pace.

"No time to lose!" said Grandad. "Empty all the files into the middle. There, where the map of Pridebridge is. We're going to have ourselves a bonfire!"

They left the lights off, working by the glow of the lantern. Like grave robbers, Maddie thought. She got started, opening drawer after drawer and pulling out all the bulging manila folders. She put them on the floor and kicked them toward the center of the room. Grandad disappeared back into the tunnel, leaving the lantern on top of the nearest cabinet. He emerged a few moments later, waving a plastic bottle above his head. A clear liquid sloshed in the bottle.

"White lightning, Maddie-me-girl!" he said. "Highly flammable! Very dangerous stuff. I got it from one of the storerooms and I've had it hidden in a little niche in the tunnel wall. I carved it out especially so the stuff would always be at hand should the moment ever arise. There's nothing better to grab Lexeter's attention than a little conflagration in his beloved Greater Index Room.

"White lightning," he said, addressing the bottle, "your moment has arrived."

"But why do we want to attract Lexeter's attention?" asked Maddie. "I mean, surely we should concentrate on finding a way to escape."

"What! Just sneak out? Without saying good-bye?" Grandad scurried into the middle of the room and began sprinkling the liquid over the growing heap of spilled papers and torn files. "I think it's time we brought things to a head, don't you, Maddie-me-girl!"

"That white lightning stinks!" said Maddie.

"Ah, but wait until you see it burn!" said Grandad. He had begun to dance. Bending his knees and kicking his long skinny legs up, he cancanned from cabinet to cabinet, capering across the painted streets of Pridebridge, wrenching open every drawer and tipping a measure of moonshine into each one.

"Well, yes," Maddie said. "That's beginning to worry me too. What if the fire gets out of hand?"

"We can get out through my tunnel. At least as far as my cell, anyway. Someone's bound to let us out when they smell smoke."

"I'm not so sure, Grandad. I don't think Potts would care much if we were roasted alive."

But he was not listening.

"My tunnel, my tunnel, my beautiful, beautiful tunnel!" Grandad sang, pirouetting unsteadily. His shadow in the lamplight flailed madly across the walls and ceiling beyond.

"Grandad!" said Maddie. "For Pete's sake . . ." She was beginning to think Lexeter was not the only madman in the Tower Library.

She got no further. At that moment the door was

thrown open and the lights switched on. The sudden flickering of the harsh strip lights left Maddie momentarily blinded. She screwed up her eyes and shook her head. When she opened her eyes, Lexeter was standing in front of her, a look of barely contained fury on his face. A woman in a plaid skirt, whom Maddie knew from Keith's descriptions to be Miss Pring, stood beside him, her arms folded across her chest. Potts was behind them, with one heavy red hand clamped around the forearm of a thoroughly dejected-looking Keith.

"So, you built yourself a rat run, did you, Lemon? And what's this," said Lexeter, glancing at the files heaped up in the middle of the room, "petty vandalism?"

"Oh no, Mr. Head Librarian, sir," said Grandad, "for you, this is the sack of Rome!" He pulled out a match.

Potts stepped forward, sniffing the air. "Careful, sir," he said to Lexeter, "he's doused the place with moonshine. I can smell it."

"If you damage so much as a single page from a single report from a single file, then, so help me, Lemon, your life won't be worth living!"

Lexeter's voice was low, cold, full of menace.

Grandad Lemon struck the match. It flared into flaming life. Everyone else took an involuntary step back.

Grandad stood, the burning match held between the fingers of his outstretched hand.

"Let Keith go!" Maddie blurted out. "Let him go. He had nothing to do with any of this."

"Oh, yeah?" Potts stuck out his chest. "We only caught him trying to pick the lock on your cell door, trying to let you go." He shook Keith roughly by the shoulder. "You've had it, kid," he added cheerfully.

Then Grandad Lemon dropped the match. A sheet of orange flame leaped up like a springing tiger. Potts shouted, Keith covered his eyes, Maddie gave a squeal, and Miss Pring screamed. Grandad let out a peal of manic laughter. Lexeter stepped forward.

"Mr. Potts," he said flatly, "we need to put out this fire at once. If you wouldn't mind . . ." He nodded toward the nearest wall. Potts looked petrified, staring at the hissing flames.

"The pipes, man, the pipes!" Lexeter shouted.

Potts shook himself like a dog coming out of water and rushed for the wall.

"Stop him, Maddie," roared Grandad Lemon. Maddie shot her grandad an exasperated look. Potts reached the wall-mounted radiator. He bent down and, with a bellow of exertion, wrenched the connecting pipe away and bent it around toward the sheet of flames in the center of the room. A jet of water arced through the air, hitting the base of the flames. Black smoke billowed up from the extinguished fire. Everyone in the room began coughing. Grandad Lemon sank to his knees, clutching his scrawny chest. Maddie knelt beside him.

"Are you all right, Grandad?" she said.

"It's all over, Maddie," he said bleakly. "The fire's out. He's beaten us."

Lexeter had taken a handkerchief from his top pocket and was holding it up to his nose and mouth. He lowered it for a moment, wafting at the smoke with his free hand, and called over to Potts.

"Very good, Potts. You'd better see to getting the water turned off. We don't want to cause a flood, do we?"

Potts turned to go but then he stopped in his tracks. A great rushing noise had begun to fill the room. A heaving, hissing, gushing sound growing louder and louder. The floor shifted queasily under their feet and the polished floorboards in the center began to heave and buckle. Grandad Lemon looked up, his eyes wide, mouth agape. He gave an astonished laugh.

"You can get the water turned off if you want to," he said. "It won't do you any good, though. The damage has been done. You hear that?"

The bubbling roar was growing louder, accompanied now by the groaning of timbers in the sinking floor. "It's that underground river I found, down below the library.

It's flooded at least once a year since I finished my tunnel, but I've never heard it sound like this before. From the look of your floorboards, I reckon it's finally washed away the foundations from under this Greater Index Room of yours, Lexeter."

They all stood transfixed. The first of the filing cabinets began to slip along the tilting floorboards.

"Well, Mr. Head Librarian?" said Grandad. "How does it feel now that the earth's about to swallow you up?"

Chapter 19

With a sickening crack, the floorboards suddenly caved in, throwing everyone off their feet. The noise of the flooding river increased in volume and the powerful smell of silt and wet earth filled the room. With a jolt, the whole floor sank about a yard. Immediately, water gushed over the buckled and splintered boards.

Maddie struggled to her feet. The water was up to her waist and rising. She looked for Keith. He was floundering, slipping over in the swirling brown water. Maddie waded over to him and took his hand. They pushed through the flood and reached the wall. The radiator with its torn pipe now dangled at chest height, bolted to the wall where the floor level had been before the collapse of Grandad's tunnel.

"Hold on here, Keith," she said as she guided his hand to the pipe, "and don't let go!"

Then she looked around for Grandad Lemon. She couldn't see him. But she saw Potts, the water almost over his head, shouting across at Keith, shaking his fist.

"You've had it, kid, you've really had it now!"

And there was Lexeter shouting at Potts and Miss Pring.

"We must retrieve these files immediately! Immediately, do you hear?"

Miss Pring was snatching up sodden papers as they swirled past her.

"The filing cabinets! Secure them at once!" screamed Lexeter.

The cabinets had begun to move, to float, to bob and rock in the heaving waters. Potts and Miss Pring both swam for the floating cabinets, and grabbed one each. But the files and all the records held in them had been swept out and were churning around and around the room, turning the surface of the water into a scummy mass of disintegrating paper.

The water began to heave and swell, slopping restlessly against the walls. A river was flowing through the room, bursting up through potholes and underground fissures newly uncovered by the surging flow to cover the miniature floodplain of the Greater Index Room, then diving back down through the remains of Grandad's tunnel on its relentless, underground charge toward the sea.

All the wooden filing cabinets were afloat now, including the two that Potts and Miss Pring were clinging to. They spun around and around on their bobbing cabinets. Miss Pring's expression was frozen in a severe frown as she tried to maintain her air of icy superiority despite being whirled around. She clung to her cabinet, silent and furious. Potts, however, gave a great bellow.

"Look out! The current! It's sucking us in!"

He was white as a sheet and his waterlogged hair had sagged and collapsed over his scalp.

Potts and Miss Pring spun around, faster and faster, drawing ever closer to the foaming mouth of the collapsed tunnel until at last the water swallowed them both up, one after the other, with a terrible shuddering gulp.

Lexeter had paid no attention to the fate of his minions. He was still swimming, keeping close to the sides of the room, struggling against the blind force that was slowly sucking him under the water.

"Potts! Pring! Where have you gone? Desert me now and I'll make you suffer for it!" Lexeter was shouting, his voice shrill and harsh, like the shriek of a seagull, full of violence and despair. He was making for the door, swimming with desperate, powerful strokes, heading for the safety of a wall he could cling to until the flood had abated.

Then a bedraggled head broke the surface, with two dark eyes blazing out through strands of long white hair. It was Grandad Lemon. He threw his bare arms around Lexeter's neck.

"Let go, you meddling fool! You dare to defy me, Lemon! You'll never see the light of day again, do you hear?" Lexeter shrieked and cursed as Grandad hauled him back into the center of the room. The pull of the current took hold of them and sent them spinning around in ever decreasing circles, locked together in one last, desperate fight. Maddie and Keith watched helplessly as the two men struggled in the swirling water, rolling over and over in a tangle of flailing arms and legs.

Just as they reached the water around what had once been the mouth of the tunnel, Lexeter somehow gained a foothold. He laughed, wild and high pitched, as Grandad Lemon was swept past him. But then the last and heaviest of the filing cabinets, finally lifted into the torrent by the sheer force of the water, came sweeping down toward him. Lexeter gave an astonished squawk as the cabinet hit him. He was sent hurtling down into the darkness at the center of the tunnel. He let out a final anguished, gurgling cry that seemed to echo around the walls of the flooded room, and then he was gone.

Maddie, hanging on to the radiator with one hand and to Keith with the other, managed to resist the pull of the water. The water level was falling, the current was losing some of its strength.

"Stay here, Keith," she said, and pushed out away from the wall, heading for the spot where she had last seen Grandad. She heard splashing. It was Keith, swimming doggy-paddle beside her.

"I'm going with you, Maddie," he said. She knew she would not be able to stop him.

The water was slowing now, but Maddie still felt it pull against her body, trying to drag her into the underground depths. Keith clung to Maddie's back and she inched her way forward.

"I think I can see something, Keith," she said. "Something white, under the water."

Maddie reached out. She felt rough, bony fingers close over her hand and saw the white tendrils of hair floating around Grandad Lemon's drowning face. He had found a handhold at the lip of his tunnel, but was clearly only seconds away from letting go and being swept away to share the fate of Lexeter and the others.

Taking a firm grip on Grandad Lemon's hand, Maddie leaned back and pitted her weight against the ebbing strength of the underground river. For a second or two, the river struggled, fought against Maddie, pulling at her legs, pushing against her back. But then the pressure suddenly broke. With a great bubbling splash, Grandad Lemon burst up through the surface of the water and flopped himself over Maddie's shoulder, coughing and spluttering, his chest heaving.

Supporting the old man between them, Maddie and Keith waded toward the door. The water level had fallen to around waist height. The life had gone out of the river. Garbage and the occasional page of now illegible notes still swept around the room, but the pace was sluggish. The strip lights overhead, which had somehow remained on throughout the watery invasion of the basement, now fizzed and spluttered and crackled out, plunging the area into pitch darkness.

"Make for the wall, Keith," Maddie said. "We can follow it round to the door." Keith gave an exhausted grunt by way of acknowledgment. They sloshed blindly through the flooded basement, dragging Grandad Lemon with them. He stumbled along between them, tripping and muttering and generally making things difficult. They reached the door at last. Keith scrambled up, back to floor level, with Maddie clasping her hands together in front of her to provide him with a foothold.

For Grandad and Maddie, climbing out of the room was more of a struggle, but, with Keith's help, they both managed it.

Out in the flooded corridor a ghostly light filtered down from the ground floor at the top of the stairs. In the pale glow they saw that the surface of the water was rippling with movement.

"Look, Maddie!" Keith said. "Fish!"

There were hundreds of the tiny creatures, wriggling in the water. Their bodies glowed with a phosphorescent inner light, their bones and organs outlined inside them like living X rays.

"There's something strange about their heads," said Maddie. And then she realized. "Ugh! They've got no eyes!"

"They must come from the underground river," Keith said. "The one *he* said caused the flood." He looked at the old man lolling at his side, one long, skinny arm draped uncomfortably across his shoulder. "They must have evolved without eyes because there's no light at all down there."

Keith paused. "Maddie," he said, "is this really Grandad Lemon?"

Maddie smiled. "Who else could it possibly be?" she said.

Chapter 20

As they dragged themselves up the basement stairs and out of the water, Grandad Lemon began to come to his senses. He still needed to keep a steadying hand on Maddie's shoulder, but he was able to stay upright and use his legs with more conviction.

At the top of the stairs stood three young men of identical appearance. All of them were pale-skinned, with tangled mousy hair falling over wide foreheads. Their eyes were large and round like those of a nocturnal mammal. They were gathered in an awkward huddle, staring solemnly at their shoes.

"Who are you?" demanded Grandad Lemon, who

was recovering rapidly. The little group flinched visibly at the strident voice of this filthy, dripping old man.

"They're the deputy librarians," said Keith, "from the first floor."

"You never told me they were triplets," Maddie whispered to Keith.

"You never asked me," Keith said.

Maddie was about to take Keith to task for leaving out this curious fact from his description of the Tower Library, when one of the pale young men took a hesitant step forward. He cleared his throat tentatively.

"Actually, you know, we're not really librarians at all," he said. His voice was a feathery whisper. "Lexeter owns us, and we have to do what he says. Um . . . is he gone?"

"Lexeter?" said Maddie. "Yes, he's gone."

The three men turned to one another with twitchy smiles and little jerky hand movements.

"And what of Potts? And the terrible Pring?" their spokesman asked fearfully.

"Gone too," said Maddie. "All sucked away into an underground river, along with all the files in the Greater Index Room."

The pale trio let out a long sigh. Then, as one they lowered themselves shakily to the ground and knelt solemnly before Maddie, Keith, and Grandad Lemon.

"Oh, get up, you silly people!" said Maddie. "And explain yourselves, for Pete's sake! How do you mean, Lexeter owns you? And what happened to the real deputy librarians?"

"They're all locked up in the Upper Tower rooms. With the overflow fiction index and the Mills and Boon books with the missing pages. All the real deputy librarians are up there, and that nice lady who says she's the police chief's daughter and that fellow that's always writing on the walls.

"And we all *do* belong to Lexeter. Quite literally. Our parents owed a great deal of money. They were desperate. They sold us to Lexeter on our sixteenth birthday. He drove a hard bargain, though. All three of us for the price of two. Mom and Dad promised to buy us back as soon as they returned from Las Vegas, but that was ten years ago." The three brothers all gave a wistful sigh and looked at the ground.

"Ten years!" Maddie sniffed, unimpressed. "That's not so very long. I've been indoors for thirteen. What did you do here, anyway?"

"We had to make it look as if the library was still working," one pale triplet said. "We used to send out requests for books we already had to one library, and then send the same books to a second library, who would send them to the first, who would send them back to us again. And, of course, no one ever read the books at all.

Mind you," he added, "it meant we could keep the shelves nice and neat."

His brothers nodded and murmured in agreement at this.

"And then," he continued, "after Lexeter had gotten the council to agree to him taking charge of sorting the town mail, we had to do that too: going through all the letters, steaming them open, reading them, looking for any secrets Lexeter could use against people, and writing them down in special code. But now he's gone! We're free! You saved us!"

"That's all very well," said Maddie, frowning, "but you knew that Lexeter, with Pring and Potts, was keeping innocent people prisoner. That he was trying to gain a hold over the whole town. That he and his two side-kicks were all power mad fruitcakes of the first order, and yet you continued to work here. You didn't even try to stop them!"

There was a tense silence.

"Er . . . we did scrape some letters off Miss Pring's door," said one of the triplets. "It made her very angry."

"Pathetic!" snapped Maddie. "My grandad was locked up in a basement for years and years and years because he stood up to Lexeter. And all you could manage was to scrape a few letters off a door!"

"What else could we do?" The triplets all shifted from

130

foot to foot, eyeing the floor miserably. "Lexeter owned us! He had a receipt and everything."

"Maybe I was a bit hard on those triplets," said Maddie. All three brothers had gone scuttling away to release the other prisoners from their cells in the Upper Tower. Maddie, Keith, and Grandad Lemon had not gone with them. They were sitting on the steps outside the Tower Library. The storm had passed and the skies had cleared. The sun beat down on them, and steam rose from their sodden clothing.

"After all," she went on, "Lexeter did have a real talent for scaring people into doing what he said. He scared me so much, I didn't leave the house until the other day, just because, years ago, he told me not to!"

Grandad Lemon shrugged.

"Here are your matches back, Maddie," he said, passing her the soggy packet. It felt soft in her hand, on the point of collapsing in on itself.

"It'd be nice to keep these as a souvenir," she said, "but I suppose I ought to return them to the owner. Keith? Could you run over to that used tire shop on the main road and give the man back his matches?"

"Okay," said Keith, and he trotted away, the matches squashed into a ball of soggy cardboard in his fist.

Grandad sighed. "I wonder what I'm going to say to

your mom." He sighed again. "I've got a lot of lost years to catch up on, Maddie."

"Me too," she said.

Grandad Lemon smiled.

"It's like we both just got out of prison, isn't it?"

Maddie nodded. They sat in silence, letting the sun dry their clothes.

A sudden swish of wings and a clamor of honking cries sounded from above. A flight of geese passed over, heading for the river.

"Wow," said Grandad, "look at that sky!"

They both gazed up into the endless blue.

About the Author

Thomas Bloor was born and grew up in London. As a young child he experienced insomnia, to which his father responded by reading to him, sometimes far into the night. His favorites were short stories by James Thurber, and C. S. Forester's Horatio Hornblower books. Soon he enjoyed making up his own stories.

Mr. Bloor was employed for a time as a school librarian, but now teaches children with special needs in a junior high school. His hobbies include painting, sculpting, making short films, and playing cricket. He and his wife and their two daughters live in London.